# We Are

# Almost

# Always

# On The

# Verge

# We Are Almost Always On The Verge

## Kilian Betlach

MUTINY PRESSINGS  SAN FRANCISCO

These stories are works of fiction. References to real people, events, establishments, organizations, and locales are intended only to provide authenticity, and are otherwise used fictiously.

Published by Mutiny Pressings/ San Francisco, CA

A version of *Used To Be That My Head Was Haunted* did not appear in Instant City. A version of *You're Doing It All Wrong* did not appear in Zzzyvva. A version of *Fourth First Day* did not appear in McSweeneys. A version of *Fifty-One Minutes* did, in fact, appear on the blog Teaching in the 408. Portions of *Pending a Full Inquiry and Final Resolution* appeared in private correspondence with the woman who absolutely shattered the author's heart, an organ which, admittedly, had become somewhat vulnerable at the time of its shattering—a mistake much of pop music assures us will never again be repeated.

Cover photo: *Mike Khavul*
Cover design: *JM Holland*

ISBN:
978-0-615-41608-3

For Jim O'Sullivan

I think I want you to like the things I write
more than anyone.

"Smothered up in gauze, the sky's
        been healing for a week or

two, conserving its basin of gruel.
        The shops have closed

in sympathy. The ferry's ministrations
        barely mark the hour. And just

when we'd convinced ourselves that
        beauty unsubdued betrays

a coarsened mind, the fabric starts
        to loosen, lift…"

                        —Linda Gregerson
                        *Verenna*

"The world breaks everyone, and afterwards
many are strong in the broken places."

                        —Ernest Hemingway
                        *A Farewell to Arms*

Used To Be That My Head Was Haunted

Fifty-One Minutes

Late One Summer

What Comes Next Is Far Less Clear (I)

Kudzu

You're Doing It All Wrong

What Comes Next Is Far Less Clear (II)

Pending a Full Inquiry and Final Resolution

What Comes Next Is Far Less Clear (IV)

Truth-Couch

Fourth First Day

What Comes Next Is Far Less Clear (IX)

We Are Almost Always On The Verge

# Used To Be That My Head Was Haunted

I looked up and she was there.

She hadn't been there—not for some time, not through all the days of my waiting. Not there when I looked for her everywhere. Everywhere, that long stride and short hair, knowing we shared this seven-mile city (the only sharing we still did).

Not there when I would endlessly picture run-ins on the street, at the park, on BART (Montgomery stop, middle cars, especially if I was coming home late). Imagine it: eye-contact and a slow walk over, initial awkwardness blooming into that connection of old. I planned for this everywhere I went, ready with a hundred ways to build that re-spark into a John Hughes moment, kissing by the cable car turnaround as tourists whooped and taxis horns blared.

It never happened, and never really came close. And still I never stopped trying, flavoring every small thing in my life with this dash of collapsed hope.

For a very long time I did this.

Then came a day where I had almost stopped. Stopped trying, stopped waiting. I was at the one-cup-at-a-time coffee place I never went to anymore, the place we used to meet up sometimes, where we would get post-run coffee every Sunday morning. I looked up and saw her perched on the chair across from me, wearing these foxy new glasses and something that looked like a smile.

"Hi, Los," she said.

I put my book down.

"I was sitting in Dolores the other day," half-pointing over her shoulder, "and I started writing this to you. I've been carrying it around, and I don't know why, and I don't get it, but then I walked in and saw you."

She smiled that little smile, and took an envelope out of her purse. My name was written across the front. I saw myself reach for it, that disconnected point of view thing happening, and then she was walking out the door.

Stacey and I met one night through friends of friends. It was one-part dinner party (because we were getting old), and one-part drunken mess (cuz we weren't old yet). I remember her skinny jeans and long black top, the over-sized green stones in her necklace. I remember staring at the curve of her throat.

There were no famous first lines, no meet-cute story we'd endlessly retell. Just introduction and the walk-through of back-story (people we both knew, places we'd grown up or gone to school, degrees we'd earned that bore no connection to our current jobs). That night it didn't feel even a little difficult or uneasy. My stories flowed into hers, and her tales flowed right back. We couldn't stop talking. All night we talked, a swerve through the apartment, kitchen to hallway to couch to the over-stuffed chair in the corner where I stood and she perched on one arm, letting her knee brush against mine just one too many times to be accidental.

We couldn't stop talking, except once when I caught her staring, and the look in her eyes stopped me cold. Her knee touching mine, and that look in her eyes.

When the party began to die down, there was talk about going to bars or going to bed, and we walked down the hill and sat on the stoop of her building. And talked. This is what I remember most about Stacey. How we never shared an awkward silence, or a pause that could not be filled with stories or thoughts or tales. All those easy words that only seemed easy because it was Stacey, and because it was me. It was like this from the beginning, the party, and later, the walk to her place, sitting out on the steps, one of those warm San Francisco nights you wish would never end. I kissed her, and put my hand on her leg.

"Slowly," she said.

Before she went inside that night, she typed her number into my phone.

"You will make use of this," she said. "Soon."

I did.

Los,

This will be disjointed.

I have no agenda here. Maybe no right to try even if I had one. This is the third piece of paper I've used. The first two are in a crumpled little ball.

God, Carlos, I'm sitting on my blanket in the park, and I don't want to people-watch, and I don't want my book, and I keep remembering your line about not having the energy to find other people's dogs fascinating. That happens a lot, remembering you. You come to me, I'd say, at least once a day. Sometimes more. I hear your voice in my head, or see one of your gestures in somebody else. Then I'm immobilized with you.

*There are times when I'm struck by something I need to share with you, and I turn and start talking before I remember that you aren't here anymore. Do you understand? I'm hard-wired to expect you here, ready to get me completely, and I start talking. Sometimes I'm alone, sometimes with other people, and I start talking. Then I have to stop, because the words are for you.*

*Do you get it?*

*~Stacey*

A week after Stacey handed me her letter there was a blank CD in the mail. Windows opened a word doc, a Pixies song, and a folder of pictures (*Sunday evening, bedroom mirror*). I played the song on repeat (*"What changed? What cha-anged?"*) and clicked through Stacey's digital self-portraits. Her hair was lighter and choppier than I remembered, her complex smile exactly the same. Her breasts and the freckle triangle on her right cheek were exactly the same.

I read the end of the letter five times.

*All my mornings start with the sun pouring through the windows, the alarm from my phone, curling beneath the covers and trying to interpret my dream about you.*

The next week there was another CD. Two weeks later, another one. They came in these $2.75 United States Post Office approved mailers. Microsoft words, thematically relevant song files, and a new set of pictures every time.

"What do you do with all this?" I asked my buddy Hector, out drinking. "What'm I supposed to do?"

"Man, fuck this bitch."

"Seriously."

"Shit. I feel like I'm supposed to spit on the floor. Y'know? She comes up in conversation, I spit on the floor."

We were at The Page, and we were drinking whiskey, and it was loud.

"I don't know what to do on this one."

"Whaddaya want? You want her back?"

"I don't know, brother. I'm a little lost, and all this cryptic shit isn't helping."

"Man, fuck this bitch."

"Gimme something else."

Hector sighed. "You called her?"

"Voicemail."

"Text her."

"No response."

"None?"

"Naw. It's all strictly literary."

"So write her."

"Can't. There's no return address."

"She leaves it blank?"

"Yeah, and get this shit. No postage."

"What?"

"There's no postage on the envelopes."

"What—she's hand-delivering?

""Yeah, I think she's walking up to my place and slipping shit in the mailbox."

Hector drank his whiskey. "Los, man, this bitch's impressive as hell."

He spit on the floor.

It finished because one of our favorite spots was Yelped so many times you couldn't get a table in less than an hour anymore. It finished as we waited. It finished because I couldn't wait.

We had begun seeing each other a few times a week. Coffees turned into dinners, into drinks, going back to one of our apartments. We were always falling asleep together in the beginning, literally passing out after hours of talking and making-out and talking. We were like a PG-13 slumber party. We waited to have sex without really talking about the fact we were waiting, but waiting nonetheless, longer than either of us had ever really waited before. My buddies assumed the exact opposite, and I did not correct them.

I remember it like the montage scene in every romantic-comedy: Picnics in the park, hiking in Point Reyes, caching a show at Bottom of the Hill, and hours of kisses, these amazing kisses that swelled into little gasps of unbelief. It was almost more than I knew what to do with, this reinvention of kissing. When we'd say goodnight I'd walk back to my car with a teenaged giddness swirling in my stomach, this desire to over-share with strangers.

"I'm making-out with the coolest girl ever!"

Then my lease expired and Stacey's roommate brought home one too many coked-out SOMA dudes, and we moved in together.

That stretch of time, looking for apartments, evaluating neighborhoods, envisioning furniture arrangements and floor plans, that was the happiest I think I've ever been. At first all we could talk about was industrial warehouse space, wood-floored and high-ceiling'd. We wanted to soften the edges of a rough loft. We wanted to refurbish and recreate, make rooms with bookshelves and strategically hung curtains. How could we be this old and this hip and not live in industrial warehouse space? It was implausible. It was absurd. We would live in indsutrial warehouse space, learn how to install a shower and a toilet main. We would.

But then we stumbled across a one-bedroom on Dolores with big windows and real closets. It was that quasi-mythical San Francisco apartment, perched on the edge of a hill. We dropped the idea of a post-industrial Potrero oasis and jumped on it.

For months we spent every weekend in this slur of morning runs throught the park, more challenging runs through IKEA, and fluid afternoon sex. My buddies made the standard jokes about Bed, Bath, and Beyond.

Once we settled, I would always try to get home first, fighting the mess of Mission parking so I could be there when Stacey walked through the door, breathless always, because she could nor climb stairs without sprinting, simply couldn't. This was my favorite thing, watching her fling the door open, her face flushed from the three flights, inevitably carrying a half dozen things (Timbukt2, purse, fruit from this one particular streetfront market she'd developed a bizarre allegiance to, BlackBerry, wallet, Nalgene). She'd get a foot inside the door and then I'd rush up and knock everything out of her hands. Knock them out of her hands like some fourth grade bully.

I wanted no holds on her from anywhere else. I wanted her disencumbered with the outside. I'd slap things out of her arms and then step over them to kiss her, putting my hands on her face.

"You have to stop doing this," she'd say, pulling me close and putting her mouth on mine. "You have to stop."

Something broke that Thursday at the Front Porch (back when the original chef was there and it was still good). No reservation, sitting in the chill, drinking Red Stripe tallboys. She leaned toward me over her crossed legs, holding the bottle tight against her, and there was something in that image, beautiful Stacey, the place where all my ladders start, something that paralyzed me. She was sitting there because of us, because of me, and the sight of her grabbed hold and dug deep. I swear the blood-flow stopped.

I saw in time-lapse photography, the days sped up and swooshing in fast forward. I saw this rip-chord move through the months, through the years. I saw us together and strong, dropping much of our hipster ways and growing further into ourselves. The bigger apartments and serious furniture, professionally framed photographs on the walls, less black in the closets. A wedding near the sun and the sea, an expatriation to big-tree East Bay neighborhoods, children, less hair, more fat, growing old together in chairs and on couches, in kitchens and backyards.

I wanted every tiny bit of it.

She saw it, too.

Somehow she could see the reels I'd made of the future, saw my open-armed approval of the whole thing. She straightened and her eyes grew large, than narrow.

"Oh no, Los. No, no."

Then she was standing and leaving and stopping near my shoulder, and then she was turning the corner, disappearing into the press of Mission Street. The next day I tried to get home first, but she had been there ahead of me, and all the rooms were half-empty.

After, came the waiting.

And after, came the looking.

The city had swallowed Stacey, and she lived in its belly. No amount of calls or texts, no emails, no visits to her friends, no lingering stalking standabouts outside of her just-off-Market office could disgorge her. I thought I saw her everywhere, double-taking with neck-snap speed, over-staring at strangers, following random women long enough to disconfirm it (no that's not her).

I became a believer in the higher power of the chance encounter. In the Church of the Random Run-In, I sat in the first pew. Riding the BART cars she liked, running her favorite city routes, buying coffee in her part of the Mission, not my part of the Mission. And was that her sitting outside of Berretta? Double-back and see (but man oh man, act casual).

There was no communion in the Church of the Random Run-In. She had disappeared, and the days of my waiting became weeks, and then months.

It was only when I started to stop, started to give up my faith, it was only when I had stopped looking down the hill at Dolores every morning hoping she'd be running back my way, only then did I see her, leaning over my handmade cup of coffee and offering me an envelope.

Then the deliveries began, and I began a new kind of waiting.

I felt every minute pass.

The fifth CD delivery was overdue on the day I came home and saw Stacey. She was sitting on those little recessed stairs that led up to my apartment, the ones that used to lead up to our apartment, holding a now-familiar United States Postal Service approved CD mailer between her legs.

"Every time I come by to give you one of these, I hope you'll catch me in the act."

She twirled the enveloped between her fingers.

"I figured you'd catch me eventually, but I couldn't stand the waiting. The waiting," she said, "has been awful."

She was already rising a little as I walked over and grabbed her wrist. I pulled her up the stairs, through the security gate, and into the apartment. I spun her to face me, and then I slapped the padded envelope out of her hand.

We were quickly naked. It was messy, and forceful, and should not have felt this easy. There should have been some hesitancy, not just these clean movements, the sharp slap of skin on skin, and the crunch of a CD beneath my foot. Her wrist was in my hand, bent behind her, pinned against the small of her back. Stacey and I. These were the seeds she'd planted with her letters and songs. It was not a resumption, and it was not unbeautiful.

Here we were again, like this again, the whole thing weighty with everything that remained unsaid.

Unsaid still.

Untalked out. Still.

Me and Stacey! This was her and this was me, who had never stopped talking, never grew tired of hearing every thought, every slice of information. We had never failed to take joy from the exacting explanation of our days. All the details, all the time, that drill down to the core of everything. Until the night she left, leaving everything untalked and unexplained. She'd given me nothing to hold on to, just the eloquence of disappearance, and her body here, now, pressing back against mine.

"You needed... this," she said. "From me."

I didn't say anthing. But I kept hold of her wrist the entire time, and when it was finished, I let her go.

# Fifty-One Minutes

You will need to get used to the bells.

This is what you wanted, right? What you've worked for? Why you took those exams and wrote those papers? Then you will need to get used to the bells.

It wasn't so long ago you were in college, those halcyon days of glorious waste when you refused to abstain from anything, when you did nothing in moderation or with restraint. There were wide expanses of free time then, entire pristine prairies of it. They weren't so long ago, those days and those prairies, but you have moved far, far beyond them. Now, your life is divided into these fifty-one minute chunks. Three-thousand and sixty seconds, one interval after another, bookended by a dull tone that is not, really, the sound of a bell.

This is not what the hourly tolling of your gothic towered college sounded like. Those were bells. This is a blank tone not unlike the sound your building's front door makes, that automatic buzzed-in noise.

Here are your six fifty-one minute chunks. Five for teaching; one for "prep." This prep time is when you drink coffee and then pee out coffee. It is also when you read emails from friends who don't have real jobs. Not like your job. You can tell who has graduated onto a legitimate job by the email. Everyone you know who works in finance or marking or fields somehow more nebulous than either finance or marketing, these friends write long, intricate emails. There are frequent links to youtube clips and whatever ironic web site has gone viral, links you can't open because the District's firewall blocks pretty much everything that isn't gmail. And sometimes blocks gmail. You feel a guilty panic every time you forget about the firewall and click a link from one of your artificially employed friends, immediating ex-ing off the screen and hoping no one is monitoring this—no thick-necked cyber-security guards in dark rooms whose sole purpose is keeping track of how many times you generate the *blocked by websense* screen on your District-provided laptop.

When you have the time to reply-all, some friends distinguish themselves from the rest by replying-all to your reply-all in an incredibly short time span. Like, within 153 seconds. This is especially remarkable given the inclusion of a thematically relevant link from Craiglist's Missed Connections section you won't click because you know it will only trigger that *blocked by websense* screen. Again.

All other fifty-one minute chunks are reserved for teaching. Please remember that the bells are in charge, not you. The bells decide beginnings and endings, not the extent of work completion, which sometimes takes many different sets of fifty-one minutes; and not the desire to send kids packing, which sometime takes less than two minutes. Atonal chime and they burst out of rooms. Atonal chime and they drift toward the next room. One of those rooms is your room, where you are expected to teach them things. They sit, eventually, at least until the next atonal chime. Then they leave and the whole cycle begins again.

You exist within this frame, within these constraints and limitations. Fifty-one minutes. It feels indescribably alien to have an external force shape your days like this. Remember that this is what you wanted.

You will need to adjust to the commute. You live in San Francisco, but there are no jobs in San Francisco Unified, the District that launched a thousand pink slips. There are jobs in Oakland, across the Bay, far from the fog and the hills and the big window'd apartment you share with the fiancée, but very near to the kind of poverty you had only previously read about in textbooks or exposés penned by *New Yorker* staffers on extended leave. There is poverty and there are teaching jobs, so this is where you go, steering your Subaru Outback across that ridiculous bi-polar bridge and into the flatland schools where no one wants to teach, not really.

Here is what it feels like to wake up in the dark every day, never avoiding that guilt-stab when the fiancée groans that awful waking-up-too-early-to-someone-else's-alarm groan. She rolls over, maybe digging an elbow into your back, the sharpest elbow of any living adult female, digging you a good one if you are too slow turning off the blaring alarm. Don't even think about wake-up sex. The wood floors that are your favorite part of the apartment are always cold, never mind what month it is, and you shuffle to the bathroom to shower, to shave, to brush your teeth, eat vitamins, and inevitably forget to turn on the coffee maker, even though you took the time to load it up the night before.

On good days, you walk less than five mintues to your street-parked Subaru. On bad days, more. Sometimes much more. Stop for coffee and then inch through the merge maze leading to the bridge, hemmed in by the type of construction that doesn't seem to be going anywhere, ever.

Getting there takes twenty-five minutes. Getting back takes an hour. It will be almost two years before you no longer feel the urge to bitch-slap anyone who uses the phrase *reverse commute* in that hopeful lilt.

You drive, usually, in a haze of NPR and the same music you listened to in college and will probably never stop listening to. Sometimes you take advantage of the commute and time zone difference to catch up with friends on the east coast, but mostly you worry about how you will spend your six versions of fifty-one minutes. This is occasionally productive worry, and it passes for what your teacher credential program called *long-term planning.* All such planning occurs immediately after you say, out-loud, in the car:

"What the fuck am I teaching 4$^{th}$ period?"

On some days you come up with a decent enough answer. Uually, your sleep-deprived, caffeine-addled, traffic-distracted brain comes up with very little that is even in the same phylum as an answer, decent or not.

Mostly though, you think about the kids.

There are some ninety of them altogether.

They are an open wound of need and want.

You will buy granola bars and carrots and apples for the ones who come to school perpetually hungry. You stock up on pens and paper and binders for the ones who have no idea what it means to buy such items, store them in a backpack, and produce them as the academic climate demands. You plan to arrive almost ninety minutes before the first bell, because the kids will get there forty-five minutes before the first bell, and their insistent knocking, their desire to come in and use the Internet and tell you tales—this is hard to ignore. Not to mention completely incompatible with planning and preparation because you still don't know what's going to happen $4^{th}$ period.

You will plan to stay well after the final bell has atonally toned, because a different group will wander through, knocking insistently. They want to listen to the radio and use the Internet and stand awkwardly by your desk to tell you tales. Daily, they need to be ordered out of your room, often in a mock-exasperated tone that has nothing *mock* about it, often with threats of physical violence so extreme and disproportionate that no one could mistake them for serious threats of physical violence.

You say, "If you're still in this room in ninety seconds I will chew off your arms, bite your arms right out of their sockets and beat you with your arms until you *and* your arms look like the parts of the cow they don't even make hot dogs out of."

The kids laugh when you say things like this, and you're not sure how you're supposed to feel about that.

And look, here are the kids. They are this deep, deep wound. There is no free time, no mental energy, no chunk of your personal finances that cannot be poured in that wound like the most potent of hydrogen peroxides. This pouring leads to a consumption that only reinforces the pouring, justifies it, encourages it, emboldens future pourings and the expansion of pouring into a variety of other areas. There is no amount of pouring that can make the pouring stop.

You will need to educate the fiancée about the nature of this wound. And you will need to keep educating, because until you are there, doing this work, hemmed in by the bells and fighting the inarguable limits of those fifty-one minutes, this is not something anyone can be expected to understand. Anticipate this lack of understanding and do not hold a grudge, ever. Even will all your educating, she won't ever really get it.

This is not irony, by the way, your inability to educate the person closest to you during a time when you are capable of educating the children of strangers. It's not ironic, but it is achingly lonely.

Sometime in the near future you will need to educate your own damn self on the merits of strategic withdrawl. You will need to learn about the digging of trenches and the maintenance of equilibrium. About how to stop pouring quite so much all at once. Martyrs are fun to watch motivational movies about; they are no fun to share a life with.

But you can worry about that later. Most people don't get that far.

Here is how you will teach.

You will teach vocabulary and spelling and phonics. You will teach past tense irregular verbs and

persuasive essays and literature. You will teach cause-
and-effect and confirming predictions and making
inferences about an immigrant father's assumption of
bus driver authority in the American public school
system. You will teach how to read questions and
eliminate wrong answers, the difference in answering the
*why* when you were supposed to tackle the *how*. You will
teach myths and introduce the concept of authorial point
of view. You will encourage higher order thinking skills,
somehow. You will thank two students for arriving on
time. You will send a student to copy The Reality of
School essay after repeated disruptions and tell him to
use his homework on which to write it, because he
previously demonstrated he did not value his homework
as an instructional tool.

You will look around at one point and some kids
are finishing comprehension questions, some are
independently reading, some are taking reading quizzes,
some are at the library or in transit, some are testing each
other on spelling and vocabulary, and you will no longer
feel quite so very much like an imposter.

It will be life or death up there, always, in front
of the kids. Life if the kids are moving with you, getting
it, those glory moments when the hands go flying into
the air. Life even if they don't get it, but plow ahead
anyway, offering you their eerie trust, that 100%
unearned vote of confidence. Anything but that jaded
stance, heads down and hoods up, unmoved by jokes or

threats or injunctions that (for realz!) this is important stuff and you need to learn it.

Death then, fifty-one minutes thick.

Frequently, there will be a basketball game. The kids will show flashes of competence but will generally underachieve. You get into it with refs a bit, but restrain yourself, because you are conscious of your role as a leader of young men. And hey, someone write down the date, because that's the first time you ever thought about setting an example for anyone, anywhere.

Players will whine about being hurt and you want to repeat a litty ditty your own coach once told you about the difference between *hurt* and *injured*, but don't, because under the former condition it is still possible to perform a sex act with one's mother, while under the latter such activities not merely socially frowned upon, but actually physically impossible. You won't share this insight, because it is not a good idea to speak to 13-year-olds like that, even though you were spoken to like that when you were 13.

Later you will stand impatiently in the foul smelling locker room, breathing the odor of stale middle school boy sweat liberally coated with body sprays, which are not, contrary to popular belief, an acceptable substitue for a shower. You offer this mantra, to be repeated as needed: *Axe is not a shower. Axe is not a shower.*

Is it possible the locker rooms of your youth smelled this bad? There's no way they were this bad, is there?

After getting every kid out of the locker room and using that fork-key-janitor-thing to get the lights off, you will only need to go back and reopen the locker room twice. Once to retrive an iPod; once to get a math book. The forgetting of the math book will get shout-announced to you as you're closing the car door, ready finally to head home, and you really, really want to say *screw your math book* because you don't teach math and you've got a sneaking suspicion your back-up power forward probably isn't the most diligent math student anyway.

You don't say *screw your math book*.

Instead, you will praise your back-up power forward for his sense of responsibility, climb out of the car, makng the sound you remember your father making whenever he got up out of a chair. Thoughts of this new, terrifying similarity between you and your father will not go away anytime soon. Just an FYI.

When you open the locker room again, using that fork-key-janitor-thing, breathing the sour stench all over again, your power forward will realize his math book is actually in his backpack after all.

The return commute takes forty minutes, and somehow, your fellow commuters will afford you no special vehicular consideration for the day you've had, and the good work you did.

Here is how you will try to unwrap your mind from everything that has gone on between the bells, before and after the bells. You will be too tired to do anything about dinner, knowing this too-tired situation cannot continue indefinitely, but somehow not too tired to share a few witty anecdotes with the fiancée, who still finds the anecdotes witty.. You will remember not to dominate the retelling of the day.

But this was a good day, and it will be hard to disengage, especially since good days have pretty much been an endangered species round these parts.

Carlos brought a pen *and* a binder, for maybe the first time.

Leshondra volunteered to read, twice.

Berto was in school every day this week.

You actually completed a lesson in 4th period.

Marcus remembered to roll to the basket after setting the screen.

Your teacher credentialing program's rejoinder that voice-raising is a silly and ineffective means to address student misbehavior, one that becomes, moreover, self-perpetuating and useless over a remarkably short period of time, turned out to actually be experentially valid and pedagogically useful. For once.

You only forgot to take attendance during 2nd and 6th periods.

These are your seven successes, and here is how they will build upon each other, linking up like carbon molecules into endless chains. These chains are heavy and clanky, and they wind and wind and wind around your tired head. Understand that they will be hard to banish. You will be unable to stop thinking about them when the fiancée discusses something a co-worker said, unable to stop thinking about them when she talks about a new wine bar she wants to check out Friday.

You will, finally, stop thinking about them during the twenty-two minues of sex and foreplay that occur after dinner, twenty-two minutes that are thankfully unbookended by either a bell or an atonal tone. You teach in fifty-one minute chunks and you have sex and foreplay in twenty-two minute chunks. You should probably not think too much about the amount of time you spend on sex and foreplay compared to the amount of time you spend on vocabulary development and attendance taking. Comparisons like this will only make you sad.

It goes completely without saying that you should not compare the amount of sex and foreplay your have with the amount of sex and foreplay your students are most likely having.

Twenty-three minutes after you banish the thoughts of your day, they are back. They linger, these carbon-chained thoughts in this strange post-partum separation you can't seem to shake, this sense of just plain *down* that will come after every moment of minor vindication, and every little triumph, after every realization of the life and validity built into your attempts to make yourself into the kind of teacher you see in your head. And this was a *good* day. A good one.

Here is how you will lay in bed, next to the sleeping fiancée. You will not think about how different your thoughts are now, laying with an arm draped across her waist, how different than before, when you would endlessly replay the memories of kissing and touching and all the sexy whispery things she said into your ear, replaying these memories until falling asleep. You will not think of the difference between then and now because you will think of the kind of day it has been. You will think of your list of successes. You did this. Look! You did this. You worked your ass off, not terribly creatively or innovatively, but bulldog style. You moved all these kids from here to there. You will think about how incredible and important that movement it is, and how proud you are, and how happy you are that they're making progress in the arenas of academic gatekeeping and life-choice potential.

But the best part is, you like, finished all your fifty-one minutes without major interruption. Dig on that for a while.

You did good. Now do it again.

Listen. No one will ever tell you this, because that's not how schools work, but you did good. Seven things went right today, and tomorrow you will need to do it again. And the next day: Do it again. And the week after, the month after that: Do it again. In fact, for all the years of fifty-one minutes that stretch before you: Do it again.

Except really, do it better.

You think your little list of seven things is enough? You will need to turn those seven into ten, then fifteen, then twenty. You will need to have so many successes, daily, that it isn't really possible to list them anymore. This will need to happen sooner rather than later, and not just because you're cashing checks your pedagogical ass can't cash. There is, clearly, much more at stake here than a calculation of ethical/financial ratios. Do it better, and then do it better, again.

This is what you will think about as you glance at the alarm clock, those red-glow digits getting closer and closer to the horribly low number that sends you out of bed and across the cold wood floors. You will think of the ways your days have already begun to Lego-click together, this masonry of an ideal, thinking of old Celtic strongholds you visited during Junior Year Abroad, their foundations slacked in the blood of strong men, thinking of a scattering array of data-point days that stretch on without end.

Go do it better again.

This is what you always said you wanted.

# Late One Summer

The abortion was never the problem.

We were two college kids, school half-finished, armed with middle class backgrounds and public school experiences. We liked weekday movie rentals and Saturday dinners out, trekking downtown in the still-early evenings, returning wine-drunk in the blue-black night. Walking, always, letting the act feel significant. The uncovering of new places, new cafés and bistros and grilles, these were Columbus-scale discoveries.

We probably acted older than our ages. The relationship did this. We wanted it to.

Periodically, in defiance of the calendar, we would buy each other gifts. Gifts we wanted ourselves, but not in sitcom thoughtlessness or tragic Gift of the Magi sacrifices. No, there was a seriousness and effort in the giving, a desire to include and share a perspectice. Here, this explains another part of me. One of our favorite things was this cultivation of our compatibility.

We used the word *love* in hushed, reverent tones, never on the phone or in front of other people, always preceded by a first name. Complete sentences. Subject, predicate.

The abortion was never the problem. Not for kids like us, agents of our generation, girded with public school sex ed. I rounded up the money; she made the appointment. We drove to an unmarked building on a wet-hot afternoon, filled forms with life story and disposed of maybe one hundred cells. I sat in a plastic chair surrounded by stacks of magazines devoted to women's health. It seemed a good idea not to read them.

Such a small thing, really, to change so much, those hundred cells. But their removal was never the heart of the problem.

On Sundays we went to the market near downtown and strolled the stalls. We usually bought fresh fruit from the dark-skinned farmers who drove in from points north and west, where the land was cultivated, not built upon. Sometimes I'd buy flowers, and loved when she wore them in her hair. Irises and lillies. Red-purple on gold. She'd dance, holding the flowers in place, performing half-serious.

We took the fruit home, standing around the table cutting and chopping, removing seeds and pits from the juicy pulp. I have such clear memories of those Sundays, slicing the green tops from the strawberries, the knife biting, tracing the circumference of the wet fruit. Cutting a peach in half and digging out the pit, tossing it aside with a wrist-flick, a few tendrils of orangey flesh still clinging to the stone.

I have such clear memories of cutting and laughing, throwing bits of fruit at each other, stickey-wt, bumping hips while our hands kept busy. I have such clear memories. The knife slipping from the apple and the blood welling sluggish, flooding the life-lines on her palm. Across the table she held the wound out for me to see. She held the wound out like a child's discovery and when I looked up, she wept.

It was never the abortion. She made the announcement slowly, in undertones kept clean of subtext, her hand hanging loosely in mine. I kept all questions and comments focused on her physical and emotional well-being.

We came to the decision easily, guided by time, counseled by circumstance. Middle-class background, public school. It took few shortened sentences. No arguments. We knew the arguments already, and disagreed with them together. No bleak religious prohibitions gaind traction here, only the acknowledgement of our unfitness, the famous line about being kids ourselves. We discussed the future-looked-forward-to shattered by a mistake, or an oversight, or an accident—some misstep with the condom? Who knows, but we did know one hundred cells should not ruin all our lives. She said she'd make the appointment.

The knife slipped, the skin parted, and the scarlet dime-sized droplets fell in heart-beat rhythm on the counter. I hurried over to press a paper napkin against her hand, holding it like I had so many times before. Her tears and the over-flowing lifeline.

"It's not yours," she said.

That concussion dullness.

My mind hit all the particulars, the dreary pseudoscience of opportunity and possibility. I recalled the calendar of our relationship, revisiting times she was busy with something suddenly come up, that night she wanted to stay in. Those post-bar phone calls that went unanswered, no matter how many times I held down speed-dial #2. I ran through pharmaceutical inventories. Latex and spermicidal lubricants and Orthotricyclin and lambskin, rubber-glove thick Lifestyle condoms bought at some gas station because we were desperate. Standing there, holding her bleeding hand, thinking about DNA and doggy-style.

She could cry and watch me at the same time. It was over now and not because of these one hundred cells. There was no way to explain and no need to broaden our secret even if there was. Besides, she didn't owe anything to anyone. Those midnight urges for something newly different? Something not without risk? She didn't owe anyone. She said a name and I think I nodded. There was no defense here, only regret, but she knew it wasn't mine, they had not been safe. Unlike us, they had not been safe.

Did I need to know, did it matter if the guy was black?

I shook my head and said *of course not* and gave her the first of many hugs meant to symbolize something. When her hand stopped bleeding, we finished cutting the fruit. Of course not, I'd said.

The next day I thought of the movie *Rose Mary's Baby*. And the next day.

She could catch me within her laughter. She laughed like a deep-sea net dragging wide, entangling. Her white teeth flashed and her breasts shook with the effort, blonde hair a shimmer past her shoulders. You could see the laughter building and bubbling in the hollow of her throat, a throb between the stretched tendons. I tried to induce this laughter every chance I could, and then give in, drawn along with the sounds, watching her shake. Sometimes I wished we could spend our entire lives this way.

No, the abortion was never the problem, but I was haunted by a symbolism that consumed each day— the Jupiter of my private shrinking galaxy. This was an imagery that consumed me, overtook me past the point of dysfunction. Inevitable, this constant imagining of half-understood events, yellowed on the edges. I thought of *Rose Mary's Baby.* I remembered, suddenly one day, the story of Alpha and Omega, the myth of the Minotaur. Father O'Heir and his classics course.

And then I couldn't stop. Didn't matter where I was. Seventh grade slide shows on the miracle of birth, the memory of watching these, all the newly formed cells embedding in her uterine walls, never the pristine white of laboratory slides. Here were arrows of black cells parasite-clinging to her insides. Digging. A connection without consent. Out of control, this daily excavation. It increased even as we walked together in the first crisp breeze of the season, expanding in her annexed uterus.

Once, I tracked down her lover. I sat and waited, watching him come out of one building and cross into another. I noticed skin color, and a long stride. I felt this violent surge, that very male desire to leap after him and start swinging. It was easily contained and quickly forgotten, never to return. In all those long months of crippling imagining, it was the only time I ever pictured that—the sex that led to this creation, her midnight indiscretion. I wish I hadn't bothered. He was better as someone else, impersonalized. An other. The imagined sex between the two of them couldn't begin to compete with the other set of images that swelled, cresting and crashing. Yang overwhelming yin. Dark pit at the center of the peach.

It was hard to cut fruit after that.

Walking across campus, sitting through dinner. Cells are always see-through. Watch them float in some water-drop world, merrily going about their business of being the building blocks of life. Her cells were black and swarmed like Bible locust. *Rose Mary's Baby*, the loss of control.

I felt too akin to her. This was the thing, after all. Too familiar and close in the incestuous match of our pale, pale cells. The expanding pit at the heart of a peach, pale fleshy-tendrils clinging to the stone.

Walking across campus, my reeling psyche and the season gathering to a close. Awake through every night, exploding in goose-bump shivers when she sleep-brushed her leg against mine.

The abortion was never the problem. After her kitchen revelation, I awaited the end of her pregnancy the way I looked forward to the termination of our life together.

# What Comes Next Is Far Less Clear

# (I)

"Like, this whole there's two kinds of people thing is so dumb, but really, there are men who can sit alone at a bar and men who just can't," Veronica said. "Can't without looking utterly ridiculous."

Megan kind of laugh-burped, emptying the pitcher into her glass. It was not the first pitcher.

"Used to be the two kinds were you worked with your hands or you worked with your mind," I said.

"Yeah, but now it's you work or you don't," Veronica said.

"No. Now it's you work, or you *incentavize* and *enhance* the *convergence* of your *action-items*."

Everyone laughed; Mikey smiled and finished his beer. He would not say anything else for another two hours.

"The two kinds of guys are the ones who know how to fix shit, and the ones who just buy a new one," I said.

"The real difference is between the ones who can make you come-"

Everyone started laughing, some of us shouting the name of Veronica's most recent ex, and she didn't really need to finish the sentence.

"No," said Greg, and he hadn't said anything in a while. "The split is who you go after. The woman, or the guy she's with."

This didn't make a whole lot of sense to anyone and we all kind of looked at Greg. Megan started to say something, but Greg caught her off.

"You're getting cheated on, right? Maybe you know about it or maybe you don't. You see them together, walk in on them mid-deed or post-deed, whatever. Maybe it's like a big surprise, or maybe you planned it, arranged for the whole thing Hardy Boys style. So that happens, and who do you go after? No, really-" although no one had said anything. "Which way does the rage send you—toward the woman who betrayed you? Or the shit-bag who was in on the betrayal? That's the two types of men."

"What if it's no one?" I asked. "What if you don't have rage toward either one?"

"Then you're not a man." Greg said, and catching the waitress' eye, held up two fingers.

# Kudzu

*"To discover in one's hand*
*two local stones the size*
*of a dead man's eyes*
*saves no one, but to fling them*
*with a grace you did not know*
*you knew, to bring them*
*skimming, homing*
*over blue, is to discover*
*the river from which they came."*
—Christian Whiman, *Lord Is Not A Word*

Dinner was biscuits and stew made from two different meats. A heavy meal, dinner and supper both. The stew bubbled in the expansive pot at the back of the stove all day, and it was necessary to scrape away the layer of congealing gravy to reach the tastiest portions beneath. Thomas drank water from the chipped glass he liked, watching his parents eat in the yellow twilight gloom. His mother broke a biscuit and set the even portions side-by-side at the head of her plate; his father worked his spoon with deliberation.

Thomas dropped a carrot in his mouth, mush-soft and stained gray-brown. He was trying to eat in time with the dripping faucet. *Drip* and he raised the spoon. *Drip* and he chewed, *drip* and he swallowed.

His father stood to get the final beer from the refrigerator. Two with dinner, one before. He bent back over the bowl again, scraping at the filmy layer with the edge of his spoon, collecting the thickened, ropey sauce. His father would occasionally smack his lips when he swallowed. His mother cleared the dishes when his father finished eating.

They left in the truck, rust-red and muddy to the windows. In the cab, Thomas sat between his parents, watching his father's big hands on the wheel, his mother's stiff back. No one commented on the passing countryside.

The church was a converted filling station on the edge of town, set back from the country road on an incline. Two skeletal gas pumps kept sentry duty, weathered and dirty so you couldn't make out the lettering across the front or the numbered tiles in the display. The building was tin-roofed, the clapboards gone gray with age. You could see where they'd finally managed to put the fire out and later rebuilt the burnt portion, extending the structure back into the waste of scraggly pine and kudzu matting. The lot was gravel and broken concrete, full up with trucks and old Chevys.

"Musn't be hardly a seat left," his mother said, allowing a hint of wonder. "We shoulda come earlier."

Thomas looked at his father and saw a nod.

"Folks musta come clear from Milford."

His father nodded again, turning the truck round to park by the turn-off, down where the asphalt gave way to rutted dirt tracks.

His mother sighed. "Well. Been awhile since we hada regular preacher come through. That last one? With the slick hair?" And her lips drew narrow, and she pulled herself a little straighter.

His father eased down the grassy incline, letting the truck tilt down to one side. After his father climbed down, Thomas scooted out the driver's side, pausing only a moment with his body full-on behind the wheel, straightening his legs and inching them toward the pedals.

They went up the rise to the church, his mother wondering aloud whether their seats would be available, the seats they'd been sitting in for who could really remember how long, wondered if those seats would still be theirs, especially since the Braggs had moved to town and were no longer around to reserve the fourth row from the front. Crossing the lot, his mother spoke again of the size of the crowd. His father stopped and they stopped, watching the big man stare down at his boots.

"Lotta folks round here needing to be getting right with God."

More even then the press of cars would suggest, a crowd had gathered. Folding chairs stood in rank-and-file rows, an aisle cleared down the center. They numbered perhaps thirty, still more to come, sitting without speaking, looking straight-gazed at the draped card table that was the altar. Flourescent bulbs lit the place like an examination room. Someone had nailed a cross to the wall.

His mother's pace quickened when she saw their seats standing open, pushing down the row to make room for one more. He sat between them, taking note of the other worshippers.

Mr. Dale who ran the grain elevator.

Fred Watson who used to be a farm hand at the Wilson place and before with Tim Greeley.

Matty Teever who he knew to be shiftless and a drunk from hearing his mother tell Mrs. Berns when she thought he was off in the woods somewhere.

He watched them arrive, doing everything he could to avoid eye contact. Thomas didn't want anyone to see his scrutiny. See him forgetting his place. The worshippers took seats in an uneven progression until it was standing room only in the low-ceiling'd hall. He shifted his weight, rubbed his neck, caught a look from his father and took to sitting still. One of the elongated bulbs in the corner flickered sporadically, without pattern, and it hurt his eyes to look, but he kept looking over anyway. And then back at the congregation.

Randy Fullerton who worked in the garage at town.

Ben Wright who had never married, sitting with his mother, and ancient woman in hat and gloves, with deep wells where most people had eyes.

He was eleven, and they had told him only that it was time to be going.

The new preacher was young, walking through the rear door and pausing just across the threshold, younger clearly than the assembled had come to expect. An unsettledness passing.

If the preacher noticed, he gave no sign, moving completely inside and pulling the door shut behind him. It latched, the only defined sound in the palce. He wore black in the expected way, holding his hands before him and moving to stand near the altar. They watched him as he watched them, pausing a half-moment with each of those who had come, and it looked like maybe he wasn't sure what came next, what to say, next.

"Brothers and Sisters in Christ."

The preacher paused over the line. Then he opened his hands and seemed, maybe, to shrug.

"God is with you."

Someone said, "Amen."

"I say thing not because the Good Book tells me so, but because I feel it. I feel *Him*, here, now, in this room, this gathering. He has come to bless this Meeting, for are you not a righteous people who love Him, God the Almighty, and love his only Son, our Lord Jesus Christ?"

And then a sharpened glance. "Do you not love him?"

Back in the rows, Thomas saw his parents nodding, heard their response, too late to echo it now. Was that what he was supposed to do, answer what questions came?

"It is good."

And turning to face them all, the preacher said, "It is good to love our God. I tell you true, it is good to praise His name and sing those praises, for whoever does not love damns his soul. We must love, and give ourselves to love... But loving Him is not enough."

Pausing, needlessly gathering eyes.

"Our God is a jealous God, as full of wrath for the evildoer as unending love for the righteous. His anger is a great thing. Massive. Swift. His anger swells daily, as in the days of Noah. His anger grows as He sees His creation fall deeper into sin. And yet His promise to

Noah holds true: Never again will He cleanse His creation with destruction. He made this covenant with Noah and it is the ark for all sinners, the only thing that shields us from His great rage.

"And so we say Praise the Lord."

They answered him, repeating the phrase in a single voice.

"He made you a promise you did not deserve and can not earn, and yet you remain His chosen. You feel called, do you not? Called here, to love Him and fear Him. Do you feel it? The presence of His hand?"

The preacher was bending over Betty Andrews, and the question was both to her and to them all.

"I feel Him," she said.

"Do you feel the presence of our Lord Jesus, walking always beside you?"

"I do, praise His name."

"It was Eve," the preacher said, softly so that few heard, "who first ate the apple."

The preacher went to the altar, leaning one arm back to rest the tips of his fingers against the surface. "My dear little Brothers and Sisters in Christ."

Near the aisle Thomas tried not to stir. His pants were over-tight and his collar stiff and uncomfortable, but he kept still to avoid his father's black gaze and heavy hand.

"God is with you. I know, because I've seen the places where he ain't. I've seen the sin, the hand and will of Satan moving among men. I've seen men gone over to drinking and gambling. I've seen women gone over to sin, letting men who are not their husbands riot in the flesh. I've seen men and women lay like dumb beasts after nights of lasciviousness. I've seen the money-lenders in every temple. I've seen men raising false idols to bigger houses and flashy new machinery that was bought, but not paid for.

"I tell you true, when you raise a drink, this pleases Satan. When you fornicate like dogs, this pleases Satan. When you place the works of man over the works of God, this pleases Satan.

"Whose children are you? Whose would you be?"

Without really daring to look behind him, Thomas started watching the faces again. He saw hands folding in the age-old gesture of supplication, saw the nodding heads, heard the devotional refrains that soon splintered into tangents and asides, mumbling the undertones of devotion.

The preacher was exhorting them now, moving into the beginning of a pace, the timeless back and forth that held the quality of a stylized movement, decrying the lure of sin. And if it was frantic, it was not without a sense of arrangement.

Thomas watched the preacher move among the ad hoc pews, speaking of love and fear and the ugly twisting places in the hearts of men where neither could be found. The preacher was speaking, leaving his sentences open-ended in half-reference to catechism recitation. The preacher spoke and they answered, not unlike school children in their off-balance monotone lilt.

"God is here."

And they said, "He is here, praise His name."

"Praise His name."

"Halleluiah. Amen."

He watched his father's mouth rise and fall in response, but could not locate the familiar voice in the tenor of assemblage. The preacher was speaking of Satan moving among them, and he wondered at it, glancing at this mother's white knuckles, trying to find the presence of some other in his own life, a force that directed his misdeeds and took pleasure in them. Thomas tried to remember the moment right before he threw rocks at the window of the McCurdey's barn, tried to see Satan in the time he and Billy Winters stuck lit firecrackers in the mouths of old bullfrogs, cackling as they exploded. Was Satan with him then?

The preacher was speaking of barrooms and the lazy men who did not work, did not provide for their families, drank up any money they made or spent it on women. Women who were not their wives.

"I done sin!"

The voice came ragged from Matty Teever, shiftless and a drunk as his mother had told Mrs. Berns. Teever had risen, throwing wide his arms, and stumbling into the aisle. Stumbling, and maybe only partly because of the drink.

The preacher strode toward him without hesitation, footfalls ringing an even gait. "He is here, He sees your sin."

"Praise God."

"Tell Him."

"I done sin. I done drinking."

Matty Teever dropped to his knees and bent his head. They turned to watch him, uncovered metal scraping across the floor, draping arms over the back of chairs.

"I done... sin. With women. Women who weren't my wife."

"Do you love Him?"

"I love Him, I praise His name. I'm sorry for what I done."

"Do you fear Him?"

"I do, yeah."

"Do you fear His judgment at the End of Times?"

"I done so much-"

"He is here. He sees you."

"Praise God."

And the preacher dropped his hands upon Matty Teever's head, one palm flat against the temple, the other cupping the back of his neck.

"He sees you and forgives you." Turning to address the room, "He sees you very well."

"Praise God," they answered.

Smiling down at Matty Teever, the preacher said, "For who among us is without sin?"

The preacher walked back to the altar, leaving Matty Teever kneeling between the rows. He about-faced, leaning into the next question.

"Who among us is without sin? Who has not turned himself over to liquor? Who has not denied our Lord God and His son Jesus?"

The worshippers shifted, and the rustle of readjustment and reposition filled the hall. Then the preacher began moving, closer, and for a second Thomas thought he would be singled out. He didn't understand what this would mean, the focus falling to him, but knew he was unprepared for it. The preacher had moved to where Ben Wright sat with his mother, and Thomas thought maybe he wasn't ever in any danger at all.

"Have you not denied Him?"

Ben pulled his back straight as if the words were a slap. Mrs. Wright crossed herself at a fervent pitch, old skin over tendon and vein, stretched lucid thin.

"This is what I offer you tonight," the preacher said. "This is what I offer to each of you. That He is here. That He is come, and hears you very well. Do you feel Him?"

*Amens* came from the rows, choruses of p*raise-His-name*. All the personal variations and ammendments. Mrs. Wright kept crossing herself and one row behind her Mrs. Berns sat with upturned face, calling out, lips moving in a familiar pattern.

"He is here, but you must let Him in, invite Him to share communion with you as once our Lord Jesus broke bread with His disciples. He is among us as His son once walked on this Earth. But you must welcome Him, you must let Him in. Will you welcome Him?"

And there were shouts now, cries of *yes* from all corners.

"Will you welcome Him? Will you let Him in, or will you deny Him? Will you deny Him as Peter did, turning away in pride, turning away in fear, turning away in selfishness. Will you turn away? Will you deny Him? You must not, you dare not. He reaches out, and you must let Him in."

It seemed to Thomas then they were all speaking, not one voice silent, raising a din. He heard his mother repeat the line and then his father, too. *Let Him in.* Between them, looking each to each, he saw his father's gaze fixed at the preacher, saw his lips moving, heard the old man repeating the younger man's words.

"Let Him in," the preacher said. "He is here, in this room, among you. Will you let Him in?"

The cacophony was fading even as the volume rose. They had all begun to repeat the line. He turned in his chair, never mind the risk of reprimand, watching the faces from the back row, watching the burgeoning zeal of the assembled, even Mr. Dale, who never smiled and rarely said more than a few words to anybody and almost never to children, Mr. Dale spoke with wide eyes and palms skyward. Ben Wright's mother held her gloved arms across her stomach, rocking in staccato motion almost as abbreviated as the bulb still flickering in the corner. Thomas turned away as quickly as if he'd come across her without any clothes on.

"He has come to you the way He came once to the Disciples, to bring the gift of speech so they could praise His name to the ends of the Earth. Will you let Him in?"

With something like a cry, Ben Wright's mother leapt to her feet, asking Him to come in, praising His name and calling for forgiveness. The words ran together, cycled through each other and soon began to loose coherence. Syntactical fumbling. The old woman crossed herself again and again, crying in tongues, melding sounds, plosives and hard consonants—the pidgin language of fervor and belief.

He watched this as long as he could, then dropped his eyes. His mother held her clasped hands near her throat, and Thomas heard her mumbling, "Praise His name, let Him in."

Were those tears in the corners of her eyes?

"He comes to you all! He comes with Pentecostal fire to warm your hearts and loosen your tongues. Will you let Him in? You who have lived in the cold too long, stand! Here is a place of fire. Who will bear this gift?"

Fred Keller jumped up, tangling in his chair, kicking it away from him, screaming his acceptance and asking for the gift of the Lord.

In the back, Randy Fullerton took three loping strides between the rows, begging forgiveness, and affirming love, fear, and a williness to bear any gift.

The entire Andrews family was shouting with something that might have been joy, and Mrs. Andrews dropped to her knees, bowed her head, gripping fistfuls of her daughter's dress and drawing her down.

The room was filled with sound, this seismographic spike and recede of prayer and supplication. It was multi-layered, pitched at all ends of the spectrum and gaining momentum. Single words came through to Thomas clearly, sometimes entire phrases, only to be drowned by the unarticulated calls for redemption, the cycling din of faith  issued from so many throats. Thomas spun in his seat, trying to watch the preacher, but his gaze kept reeling away, hooked by the sight of each successive worshiper taken into the hand of God.

"He gives you the gift of His presence. Almighty! Powerful! Magnificent! You bear His fire in your throats! His fire pours from your mouths!"

Thomas was watching the flourescent flicker when his father stood and moving toward the altar, lurching like a man drunk. The sound was everywhere in the room at once, growing, and they were all moving now—some were on their knees, some were moving toward the altar, and he realized he was the only one who remained seated.

"Let Him in. There is nothing but God, nothing apart from the love of Him, the fear of Him. Who among you dares deny our Lord? Who would choose the cold? Let Him in, and He will fill you with fire."

The preacher came closer to where he sat among the spreading dischord. There was no way left to hope that maybe the preacher had a different destination in mind. He was headed this way.

Thomas was aware of many things at once. His father, up by the makeshift altar; his mother, leaking tears; the preacher, here suddenly, leaning toward him. From the back of the room, someone let out a joyous shout and he flinched from the sound of it.

"Love is not enough. Our God is a jealous God, a bringer of fire. Let Him in. Who dares deny Him?"

He tried to force sound. He tried to speak, to utter words, any at all, something from the litany of praise he'd heard all night coming so easily from the mouths of so many. Thomas tried to mimic their sounds. The shadow of rapture had reached him, and clearly it was time. Everywhere he heard the name of the Lord, and he tried to make those vowel-consonant combinations, those barest reduced elements.

The din grew and levled off. He tried to speak the devotional words and he could say nothing. He could not say anything.

Thomas felt the first hot tears trail down his cheeks. They were looking at him, waiting for him to speak with fire, and he could only cry. He sat there hating himself for it, and at the same time wondering if maybe they would misinterpret his tears as a profession of faith and leave him be. Maybe the tears would be enough. His father was there, standing just beyond the preacher, looking as he never before seen him. Thomas clenched his hands and he considered this, that his hands were clenched and if he did not relax, he would draw blood. Here he was, with hands about to bleed, and somehow his tongue had betrayed him.

He was weeping fully now, shoulders jerking little up-downs. Thomas strained against his muteness, filled in with high-wire tension, biting at his lower lip, hearing in some far off distant way the outburst of rapture that never came.

Later, they would walk across the uneven gravel lot, rubber soles crunching the pebbles and bits of old concrete. Headlights from reversing cars would splash them with two seconds of spotlight force. They would walk down the patchy-grass incline, climbing into the truck and sitting three to the cab. His father would drive them home on the interchange of uneven roadway, and they would not return for seven days.

The next day they would eat what was left of the stew.

When the meal was finished and his chores complete, Thomas would walk into the woods, passing without second thoughts the creek where the rocks with veins of fool's gold made him think of pirate treasure, the hollowed tree that served as a hideout, the clustered rocks he liked to think marked an ancient Indian burial site. He would walk to a place where the trees stretched their tallest and the ground below was free of scraggly underbrush. Standing there, far from where anyone could hear it, he would shout the name of God.

He would shout, and when only a partial echo came back to him, and he would shout again, mixing in the phrases he heard the night before, giving voice to the blended emotion that had failed to come erupting from his back-throat.

Out there, beneath the trees, there would be no one to hear his exaltations. No one to overshadow his words with their own. He would shout and stomp in a furious pantomime of piety, recycling the phrases, casting them into new combinations, working to recreate the force and clarity he remembered from the night before. His voice would come full and uncracked as he repeated the lines into exhaustion, making sure.

And when he finished, when he was sure, he would walk back the way he had come.

# You're
# Doing
# It All
# Wrong

*"The sad songs don't help."*
—Lucero, *Nights Like These*

No.

No, no, no. No.

Like this. Look. Do it like this.

Here is how to absorb the announcement. Don't interrupt. She has had time to choose the words she wants you to hear, this announcement. Like some kid in school, you can ask questions later. When it is later, when you've waited your turn, choose your questions carefully. Don't ask dumb ones. And don't blow it on not asking the ones that will tsunami through your head every night for the foreseeable future. Is this fixable? Was there an infidelity? To what extent was the possible infidelity a motivating factor? And just what exactly happened here? Is this actually happening? Would an impassioned plea, made here and now, placing your hands on tender and affecting body areas (but not boundary-crossing areas), do any good? Any good at all?

Here is how to leave the apartment, grabbing first your hoodie, then the corduroy coat, the one you've kept since college, the one with the pockets that open from the top. Walk to the door, ignoring her insistence that you stay. She actually insists you stay. This makes zero sense, like absolutely none, and you need to ignore it no matter how many times it is repeated. If she blocks the door, this is how to punch first your chest near your heart and then the door near her head to pretty much guarantee she gets it. Reference the pain of all this suddenly purposeless passion. Use it as a rebuttal to her absurd insistence. Really what the fuck does she expect? Whether or not she follows you into the hallway has no bearing here. What she may or may not say as you walk down the stairs has no bearing here.

This is how to carry the whiskey in the pockets of your coat, the ones that open from the top, not the sides. Drink the whiskey and wander the streets. When the bottle is empty, buy more.

This is how to return much later and sleep on the couch. Do this exactly once.

Here is how to have the worst conversation of your life. She is ready to discuss the separation of possessions. This is no longer about emotion and commitment and relationship. This is no longer about your future and her future. This is about logistics. This is about stuff. You want to say *take everything* because fuck it, you don't want to see any of this again, ever, don't want to touch the coffee-maker she used every Sunday morning and suddenly break into a fit of little high-pitched girl weeping, three weeks from now.

You do actually say *take everything* but she talks you down from this, and just the way she's so okay with the situtation, the ways she's already thought this through—it's killing you a little. The bookshelves, the table, the T.V. in your column; the bed, dresser, and chairs in hers.

You're doing about as good as anyone can reasonably expect.

There is an awkward moment by the door, when she touches your side a little and then stands there, looking. Twenty-four hours ago you would have known what to do with that look. You would have seen that look and felt that touch and thrown her across the nearest bed or couch or acceptably sturdy chair, but not today. Today, she wants a no-hard-feelings-fuck, and it doesn't matter how much you want to touch and hold and screw, how much you still believe that sex has some curative power, believe it still like some swooning teenage girl, today you stand with your not quite thousand-yard stare and do nothing. You want to get naked with her on the bed, but you know she will feel better, after, and you will only feel worse.

Besides, that's not your bed anymore, is it chief?

Right, it isn't.

And now this is how you walk up and back and through Alamo Square and completely lose your shit. This is you doing less good, but go ahead, just lose it. Choke yourself with tears and shouted *whys* and sometimes other types of noises. Ignore the yuppies and their stupid fucking dogs. Make sounds that are not words. It doesn't make it better, but it sure as hell can't make it worse.

This is the friend you call first.

These are the friends you call next.

Here is how you will talk about it. Assume a tight smile and a look-down glance, begin sentences with *yeah, you know, not so good.* It is important to develop that elevator speech version, because not everyone wants you to empty this entire bucket of shit at their feet. In fact, most don't. What they do want is to offer advice, and you discover you are not interested in advice. Or next steps. Or lessons. Or comfort. You only want to talk. Talk about it all, talk in rich detail, retrace every event and every word to the $n$th degree of awful analysis. Who knew? Shit, man. This has never been your way, the talk-just-to-talk method, and you cannot be hurt by the friends who are not equipped for this. Sure, some are, and these are the ones you call when you can't sleep, when you feel blunt and purposeless, when you're wandering your seven-mile city because you can't go back to the apartment that used to be home. She lives in your apartment, remember? You live on couches.

Here is how you learn to murder yourself with imagined situations, just kill yourself with this stuff, all of it conceived in your brain's worst-case-scenario breeding ground. There are thousands of upwardly mobile developers and real estate agents at work on this mental plot of land. They're clearing space and laying foundations. They're putting up walls and talking about landscaping. It gains cellular acreage by the minute. When you tell yourself the landscape of your imagination is improbable and absurd and nowhere close to what's really going on here, you should try very, very hard to believe yourself.

This is how to see her one more time, the last time, forever. You can't live with the regret of a last attempt gone unattempted, so you ask her to stay. She tries not to roll her eyes. You insist things are worth working on; she says you shouldn't have to work. You mention the possibility of changes; she reminds you she isn't interested in any changes anymore. Except one. Except the one with her and the door.

Here is how to sit in silence after that particular haymaker.

You could say: *I'll never forget you.*

You could say: *You're the best thing that ever happened to me.*

You could say: *I hate you for this a little, hate you, really, nibbling at the edges of everything you've meant to me, all the ways we've come to shape our lives together, into protein receptor ligand bonding, seeing not through a* me *or a* you, *not those ways, not anymore—this hate chews into all that, a tumor spreading through the ways we are changed, eating at the pride we once felt in how we changed in time with each other. This new hate.*

All these things you could say are more or less equally true.

And equally pointless.

She is sitting with her hands clasped, wearing the college team hat you never liked, staring at her tightly gripped fingers. You say nothing, but put your hand fully against her cheek, and then walk away. Your hand was on her face and she leaned into your hand. You did not imagine this.

And so now here is how you learn to doubt. Every. Single. Fucking. Thing.

This is crippling insecurity about how you communicate affections, your level of emotional availability, whether you are capable of making someone else feel special, whether anyone will ever want you to make them feel special again, how much you work, what kinds of work you do, the compatibility of you work with serious connection making, whether the work has narrowed you in a mental or emotional way, how bad your bad habits are, if you are too inflexible, if you are too flexible and unassertive, if you dropped the pointless yet compelling anger of your 20s too soon, if your interests are static and sheltered and boring and old. This is, of course, the doubt about how you look, how you do your hair and how you wear the clothes you wear, how you look when you're not wearing clothes, whether anyone would be interested in being with you in an unclothed state, again, ever. It goes without saying that here are miserable uncertainties about your mouth, your tongue, your hands, but especially, and of course, your dick.

This is how to lay awake in bed with someone else, having superimposed her face, and the muscle memory of her limbs, and all her favorite ways of touching onto the body of this other woman in a totally unfair and predictably disastrous way. Here is how to feel utterly alone in the exact moment when a vital, crucial part of your body is literally enclosed within a vital, crucial part of someone else's body. This is not next-morning regret. This is something far more present.

Here is how to move back into a half-empty apartment, the partial emptiness of which is so much worse than a complete and total emptiness. Walk through the place remembering what used to be in this spot or that shelf, that mix of appreciation and despair at the effort she has given to rearranging things prior to her final departure, all these minor movements of furniture and pictures and nic-nacs that make it seem like maybe you have been living here alone all this time. As if you woke up and none of the previous years of cohabitation had occurred. She put your old coffee table back. She replaced her curtains with the blinds that preceded them. And dusted.

You don't cry when you see the bathroom stark and clean again, devoid of her feminine clutter. You don't cry when you open the cabinet and see the condoms you used to keep in the dresser back when you still had a dresser and still used condoms, before tests and the pill.

This is when you cry.

You cry when you realize the whole place still smells like her. Smells just like the spot at the crux of her neck and shoulder, the scent filling each room, and you cry because you want to open windows and let the freezing San Francisco air blast through the half-empty rooms and chase away that last lingering part of her, and at the same time (at the same time!) you want somehow to seal the place off so you can live in the vibrant scent of her, here, forever. So, yeah motherfucker, you cry.

Here is how you live in a time of self-focus and strange acceptance, everything lateral, this new self, this damaged goods version of you, waiting to meet the woman with the potential to reduce her and all this hellish nightmare time to the level of mere anecdote—an anecdote you'll tell in bars and at dinner parties and one that you'll eventually stop telling altogether.

Here is how you wait.

# What Comes Next Is Far Less Clear

## (II)

I was watching her find clothes and put them back on. It wasn't clear to me how much I should pretend to not-watch.

I could remember really digging this moment, anticipating it, looking ahead almost. Watching a woman dress, her looking at you looking at her, that eye-lock in the mirror's reflection. The clothes were for her, but it was always a little for you, too. Dressing before going out, after work or after sex. Standing, considering, taking longer than she needed. That slow peel-off of a blouse. Lifting one leg to pull up her stocking.

But that was another room, another city. Another woman.

Tonight I'm not sure if I should even be watching at all. There's little in her hasty grabs and mirror avoidance that makes this a moment to share. She's buttoned her jeans and tucked them into those brown boots. Her bra is in one hand.

"Can I ask you something?"

She's startled a little, but hides it. She quick-smiles over one shoulder, then turns away to clasp the bra in front of her, spinning it and slipping it up over her shoulders.

"Course baby. What is it?"

"Before? When you had your eyes closed, right then?"

"Yeah?"

"Who were you pretending I was?"

# Pending A Full Inquiry And Final Resolution

**Day 8**
**San Francisco and points north**

The fires started in Humboldt.

She had left without packing, not really. No real thought put into the collection of shirts and underwear, the one pair of shorts or the jeans she was already wearing. Vickie was terrible at packing and planning things like this even in the best of times, even with the opportunity for preparation. She tried to compensate with checklists and graphic organziers, called in a consultation from one of her girls, and still made a hot mess of things. Maybe leaving like this was a roundabout solution of sorts, leaving without any of the potential build-up. No time for checklists, and no time to be disappointed when the checklists failed.

Not that it mattered all so very much.

In Humboldt everything was on fire. That's where the road curved in from the coast, that big eastward bend, leaving the Pacific overlook. That kind of road, with sheer drops and views of the white-water chop, would not be back until the state line. After the state line. Vickie drove through hills that became increasingly steep, trees that became increasingly tall and red, haze that became increasingly indistinguishable from smoke as it rolled in through the mountain passes. She never saw the actual flames, but their impact was everywhere. That yellowing in the air, stopping for gas, watching it get darker. Black coulds on the yellow horizon. Northern California was a bruise.

This wasn't what Vickie wanted, not the travel-escape she pictured as she haphazardly stuffed balled socks in her suitcase. She wanted clear horizon swallowing the winding road. She wanted hot sun on her face and her one arm hanging from the window. She wanted to earn tank-top tan lines, hair whipping out behind her like every kind of commercial, every kind of movie. Instead she got fires in the distance, this doom-haze everywhere, all those hundreds of miles north from home and out of California.

She held her breath when she crossed the state line, inhaled deep and held it like she'd been taught as a little girl.

**Day 8 (ongoing)**
**Selected text messages received and deleted without response**

**From: Jeff**
+4154872526
Baby, any news? Did you hear from the guy?

**From:**
+5104678193
Where u at

**From:**
+5104676563
Y u cut?

**Day 7**
**Oregon Coast**

In the morning the road swung back west, back to the ocean, and Vickie stopped much more frequently, not just for gas and peeing. There were all these turnouts and overlooks, exiting and swinging under the highway, that loose gravel crunch beneath the tires.

She sat on the car and smoked a cigarette, watched the ocean. Watched the waves crash against the rocks that jutted like broken teeth. She traced imaginary swimming routes through those rocks and out to sea. The coast was green and stark, like the Ireland of her imagination. And Vickie wished all at once that she'd gone to Ireland junior year. Sitting on the car, hood hot under her thighs, she wanted Ireland, wanted that experience, and felt so suddenly angry that she hadn't gone, and furious at Sarah Bigby for convincing her to go to Florence instead. Angry at herself and furious at that bitch Sarah, that awful bitch whose crimes included befriending her during orientation, and later, showing her all around Florence, and much later making her wear a not-at-all-hideous yellow dress at her Tuscany wedding. That bitch. Vickie felt robbed of something critical and immense, and it was *all Sarah's fault*. All of it. She'd rip Sarah's hair out by the roots if only she would materialize at this scenic highway overlook.

And then her anger drained away into loss. Loss because she went to Florence with Sarah Bigby neé Barnes and ate gelato and amazing five-course dinners, danced at dozens of discotechs and was pretty much the biggest make-out whore ever, instead of spending an entire semester perched on a cliff near Galloway, gazing pensively into the distance.

Vickie smoked the cigarette down and got back in the car, putting on a cardigan she didn't want, wearing it over her tanktop because the sunburn was getting worse. She refused to drive around out here with one lobster arm, and this was only a little silly, this pride. Considering.

As she headed north, 101 switched identies. One minute state-bridging highway, one minute main street running through quaint shoreline town. Vickie couldn't stop stopping. It was all her childhood summers in all these little towns. She ate top-heavy ice cream cones. She dropped into mom-and-pop seafood stands, and wanted to order the whole menu every time. Fried clams and chowder and crab cakes. Just like after her dad's softball games on those Cap Cod summers, jean shorts and two-color baseball tees and fried fish.

It didn't matter so much right then that all that was two decades and three thousand miles in the opposite direction.

The sun was going down, that time of day when everything was beautiful and driving miserable, and Vickie stopped again, pulled into a parking spot directly in front of the place, and when was the last time she had that particular experience? She ordered oysters and local beer, sat by the window, finger-tracing the countless initials carved into the aged wood surface.

She wished the middle-aged waitress, who may or may not have been the owner, she wished the waitress wanted to hear her story. Isn't that how this worked? She'd get out of the travel-stained car, all stiff-legged and blinky in the sun, and tell her tale. Just spill it. Everything. Tell about the piece of paper in the front seat that forbid her from returning to work, forbid her from having contact with anyone associated with work. Tell about the rumors and inuendo that preceded the delivery of that piece of paper. Tell about the power of a piece of paper (three paragraphs, standard business formatting) to change her life. She was supposed to tell it right? That's what was supposed to happen here.

When she lit up, the waitress, possibly the owner, said: "Put that out, wontcha, honey?"

Vickie did, waiting for the waitress-maybe-owner to drop her a knowing look, a motherly look, and draw the story out of her. She'd speak slowly, telling a parallel tale that wasn't immediately connectable, but revealing of the main issue nonetheless. Issues, actually. Plural. About how she can't go back to campus. About how she left on a Friday like any other, and then got the phone calls. About how the phone calls came first, and then the letter, after.

When she couldn't get the cap off her beer and had to be directed, twice, to the built-in opener next to the register, Vickie expected the waitress-maybe-owner to see past this discombobulated blonde(ish) moment to the issues that lay at its root. To the issues that caused all this in the first place. Instead, she went in the back.

Instead, she served Vickie's food in the ubiquitious red and white paper basket, lingering not at all. She said nothing that invited a back-story confessional.

When she finished the food and the beer, Vickie got back in the car, trying not to feel like it was her fault, like the waitress-maybe-owner had limited life-story-listening resources, and hers just wasn't worth it.

## Day 5
## Unsent postcards from Portland

Hi Katy! I'm in Portland. Loving it! Like everything we loved about Boston minus everything we hated. We should move here and own cats and eat organic and pretend to be old lady lesbians. Miss ya lots.  ~Vickie

Jeff. Hi.

**Days 7-5**
**Selected text messages received and deleted without response**

**From: Jeff**
+4154872526
I miss you baby. I get it but I'm worried and I miss you. Call me please.

**From:**
+5104678193
When r u coming back?

**From:**
+5104676563
Ill be more better. For realz…

**From: Jeff**
+4154872526
This no contact stuff is not okay.

**From:**
+5104679522
Everything is a disaster with you not here

## Day 3
## Seattle

Seattle did not feel like Portland. Portland felt like coming home. It wasn't just the superficial connectivity to the San Francisco streets Vickie didn't think she'd ever fall out of love with. And not just the all-over presence of skinny jeans and fixed gears and expensive coffee. Something more. Vickie started making friends immediately, talking to strangers in an uncreepy way. In a real way.

She ran back and forth across those bridges until her knees went brittle and her lungs burst. She criss-crossed the river in that inexplicable Portland sun, so good to be running after so much sitting, waving *hi* to everyone, and smiling, maybe, for the first time in many, many days.

Seattle wasn't that way at all. Seattle felt like being a $3^{rd}$-generation invite to a dinner party. There's the hosts, their friends, some friends of friends, and you, with your ingratiating smile and shitty bottle of wine.

## Day 2
## Email downloaded on a mobile communication device, and partially read before ultimate deletion, somewhere not quite in Spokane

I know this has been unthinkably terrible,
but I've got to think there is a way through
what you're feeling and dealing with that
lets you keep your independence, let's you
focus on what's eating at you, and doesn't
dissolve the connection and life we've been

*[scroll]*

We are not the stresses of our lives. We
don't measure ourselves that way. I am not
your work or your lurking restlessness with
everything. The circle of you and me is not
that circle. We may be touched by it, but we
are not of it. You told me once that

*[scroll]*

It's vibrant and real and truly, truly
stronger than the afflictions before us. And
when we

*[scroll]*

Yours in love and confusion and hope. Jeff.

*[reverse scroll]*

*[delete]*

## Day 2 (still)
## Off the highway, the other side of Spokane

The rest stops had free coffee and just as free wireless. It was pretty much the greatest thing ever. Did every state do this now? Or was it a home of Microsoft and Starbucks thing?

Vickie sat a damp picnic table, drank bitter coffee, looked at her dog-earred road atlas. Seattle was falling further behind her, and this was a good thing.

In Seattle, in the U-district, she had read flyers stapled to light poles and wheat-pasted to buildings, looking for a show that seemed promising. She wanted something loud. That crash and pound of drums and the guitar cranked so high she wouldn't be able to hear the lyrics. No words, just the vocal force. She wanted to lose herself in a driving *rat-tat-boom*, pushing, jostling, hemmed in a small dark space. She wanted to bounce with one fist in the air, wanted to feel that ebbing of the girl-at-a-show respectable distance, the re-press in around her. She wanted to be knocked down as the chorus hit and hauled back to her feet, yanked up before she got trampled, wanted that two-second affirming glance that meant so very much when she was Manic-Panic-ing her hair at 17, that glance that felt better and meant more than those parking lot make-outs with boys she would never bring home.

She wanted a boy, too.

A little one. Heroin-thin. With a sleeve of tattoos that was the only moderately dangerous thing about him.

They were everywhere of course, boys like that, and Vickie wanted the scrawniest of the lot, narrow hips and ribs showing when she peeled off his t-shirt. She wanted no resemblance to Jeff, nothing like his beard and strong-armed embrace. She didn't want to be held. She didn't want  swallowing arms. No. She wanted a nerdy little hipster boy to throw around, a smooth-chinned boy who would try to take charge when they got back to his roommate's futon. Try, and fail.

This was her show, Vickie's, here, now, with this boy and his jutting collar-bones. She put her hands on his throat and tried to make it make sense.

Because this thing they said she did, it didn't make sense.

It was just too far away from something she felt capable of doing. The accusation. The voice on the phone, and later, the letter. Fuck Kübler-Russ and those stages, this was all denial, all the time. Vickie dug in deep and kept coming up empty. This wasn't in her. The boy was taking her breast into his mouth and they'd read her so wrong. It prevented that deep engagement thing from happening, that wide-eyed, jump-in-with-both feet thing. She needed it. She couldn't put together a defense without it.

In college, her friend Katy had dated guy way beyond her, an absolute 10 to Katy's solid 7, maybe 8 on a great hair day. Katy would be out with him and they'd be at bars saying things like *you-gotta-punch-your-weight* and *I-love-Katy-but*. They gave it three months. It lasted a year, but when it ended it was in a shitstorm of infedility and betrayal. Not one revelation but two, and these were not anonymous violations. Not at all. Two of the same friends that professed love for Katy, and questioned the alignment and the match, took their own chances with Mr. 10 when Katy wasn't around, when the night ran long, when they were asked back to his dorm.

The thing was, Vickie shared the guilt, because she probably would've helped the guy, that absolute 10, cheat on Katy. She had it in her. She thought about what her friends did, talked about it again and again with Katy, and realized it could have been her. She was capable of a betrayal like that, and probably would've, yeah, for sure, given the right circumstances. She had hypothetical skin in this game, the guilt of potentiality. They all broke down together. They all got better together.

And she didn't know how to do that here. It was all too alien and too far gone, and it wasn't until this night, an interchangeable hipster's cock inside her, that she thought maybe yeah, okay. Maybe this made sense, reaching a hand back and slapping him, slapping him as hard as she could. One moment her hand was pushing down against his bicep, fingers splayed across the anchor tattoo'd there, and the next she was in full-force, rear-back, follow-through, shoulder-turn, hand-stinging impact.

She did it again.

It felt good, the pressue of him, the feel of his skin against her palm. It made sense to hit him. It made it make sense. This is what it felt like, hitting him. She grabbed under his jaw, and tilted his head toward her, squeezing. She kept one hand there beneath his jaw, the other above his head against the wall, and no one even tried to pretend his roommate was asleep anymore.

## Day 0
## Missoula, MT

These were not the right lasts.

Not the right ones at all.

The lasts were piling up that whole time, and she didn't even know it, didn't know they'd be the ones. Last soccer game, Saturday Academy, and Honor Roll Night. The last Lewis and Clark Discovery Project, the last oratory competition, last time through the stomach punch end of The House On Mango Street. The last essay portfolio analysis, the last time they'd read with dinner-plate eyes just how far they'd come.

Then the last, last.

Vickie wasn't ready. Maybe you never can be ready, but she wasn't even close.

She had this idea, this set of images she was playing with, maybe the beginning of an idea of how it would go, many years in the future. But this wasn't it. It wasn't time yet.

Some day, she'd walk in and the room would be stripped mostly bare, a return to its native state. The lamps would be given away, the posters gone, the better furniture passed around. She would have already turned in keys, laptop, zero period time sheets. She would take a last look before letting the door swing closed and walking into the quad to sit. She would sit on the benches they didn't have when she started, next to the trees that hadn't been planted yet. How do you leave? When you've poured so much into a place, when a place has meant so much, how do you leave?

Maybe it would start getting dark. Maybe other late-stayers would come by and they'd smile at each other ruefully, shake hands and hug, and there wouldn't be a lot to say, beacause really, what do you say?

In Vickie's imagined departure scenario, she'd sit in that quad for a long time. Then, finally, she'd untie the old-school Chuck Taylor's she wore every Friday— official footwear of hip young teachers everywhere— take those Chucks and toss them over the telephone wires, leave them to hang with some beat-up no-brand Payless shoes. Mute recognition of time very well spent.

That could never happen now.

They stole it from her.

An accusation, a phone call, a letter, and an administrative leave carefully calculated to run out the clock on her.

When Vickie woke up, before she remembered what city she was in, she remembered what period it was. Before she thought about where she was, she thought about where they were.

At the bakery at home it was zero-period, and she wanted to practice phonics and fluency. By the Seattle waterfront it was third-period, and she wanted to analyze indirect methods of characterization. On the road, later, it was seventh-period, and she wanted to work on response to literature essays. Every day at 3:30 she wished she was anywhere but wherever she was, wished she was standing in the doorway as khaki-pant-polo-shirt teenagers passed by, saying goodbye in three languages and smiling in one.

## Day -1
**The one text message that will actually go undeleted for a very long time indeed**

## From:
+5105291048
Thx 4 everything u did 4 me. Ama never 4get it.

# Day –2
# Jackson, WY

**From:** Vickie.Gang@gmail.com
**Sent:** Sunday, June 19, 2008
**To:** jeff.t.kaufman@gmail.com
**Subject:** (no subject)

It's a slow crawl through Eastern
Washington, Jeff. It's empty, empty land.
I'm eating these huge, dense Washington
apples, and driving on I-90, thinking about
how I could drive on this road for like
three days without exiting or turning, and
at the end of those three days, make a
right-left-right and end up in front of my
old Boston house. This is a crazy country we
live in, vast and immense.

In Idaho the road twists through a high
mountain pass, and I can see the storm a
mile off. It's localized at the top of the
pass, crashing and thundering and spitting
rain up there in its own little country. The
car groans as we climb, and it gets darker
until near the top it's middle-of-the-night
dark at 11:30 a.m. The raindrops are the
size of gumballs and the storm clouds feel
like they're about two feet away. And then I
hit the downslope, the rain receding, and
the sky growing light, and soon it's a

million degrees again, and I'm sweating
solidly.

Here is an important distinction between
Portland, OR and Missoula, MT, Jeff. Please
commit it to memory.

In Portland, people tell you about this bar
that's got amazing cheap steaks and
fantastic whiskey. You go, and yes, the
steak is good and $5, the whiskey is smooth
and tastes amazing with lemonade in pint
glasses. What the recommending people sort
of fail to mention is that the bar is filled
with naked women who want to shake all their
womanly parts at you. *All* their parts. There
aren't champagne rooms or VIP booths or
poles (okay, there's one pole), just naked
women and lot's of people eating steak and
drinking whiskey. But no one mentioned the
women to you: Portland.

In Missoula, I walk around aimlessly, this
college town that is like every other
college town, fairly deserted now cuz it's
summer and the kids are home. I wander into
a place sub-titled "A Gentleman's Club,"
expecting the naked women thing now in the
same way I wasn't expecting them in
Portland. I'm greeted instead with a smoky,
expansive room filled with leather-faced men
playing cards, and not one single woman

anywhere. I am like the first woman to set
foot in this place in forever maybe, and I
spin around and beat a hasty retreat:
Missoula.

Outside of town I sit up on some rocky
outcropping and watch the sun go down. The
sky is red through the clouds, and the heat
lightning refuses to quit. It comes
repeatedly, forceful, and this is just
exactly the way you would snap and crackle,
Jeff, if you were lightning, isn't it?
Sometimes the lightning is a solid white
blanket flashing up against the red sky, and
sometimes it is an impossible interwound
pretzel, these thin electric wires,
tangling. Tangling like two lovers wrapping
arms and legs and fingers around and around
each other. There is no one else anywhere.
The sun sets further and the light in the
sky fades from red to pink. Behind me, to
the east, things have that blue-black cast,
night creeping up. I sit and watch it all
for a long time, and if you think I wasn't
up there wondering what it'd be like to kiss
you, kiss you over and over beneath that
rose-red sky, the horizon all spark-lit by
lightning that does not, will not, cease,
what it'd be like to have the sparks from
your lips and fingertips mirrored by the
energy above us, if you think that wasn't on
my mind most of the night, and again the

next morning, driving south into Wyoming,
then you're just as crazy as everything
that's happened since, as crazy as
everything they said I did.

# Truth
# Couch

In those early days, the days of small pebbles that rolled and gathered speed and momentum and dislodged all other debris into a thundering avalanche, we would play TruthCouch nearly every week.

It would happen after we had eaten the dinners I was just learning to cook, served sometimes in a single large dish, clinking forks, laughing; after we had unwound with bad network television—maybe *Grey's Anatomy*, maybe *The Amazing Race*—casting ourselves into the pre-structured reality, those jokes about how they would make marketable, believable characters out of the two of us; after deep-ended kisses, long, long like only teenagers remember how; after sex or sometimes right before (but always after the nakedness), laying spooned together, laughing sometimes about the wet spots foreplay left on the fabric of the couch—my arms wrapped around her, curling up between her breasts, her arms holding my arms, knees into knees, quads behind thighs.

"Are you always this intense?" she said. "I'm for real, Foster. With other women. Are you like this? Have you been like this with... them?"

She wasn't even sort of asking about an anonymous *them*; she was asking about one particular person, and this was not a good question to answer. Not like this, laying naked like this, and maybe not at all. You avoid questions like this. You hedge, dodge, banter a subject-change. You don't tell an unvarnished truth.

Except I did. There was something that night that made me, or forced me, or guided me to tell her. To say it direct and complete.

"I want to be. I almost am. I mean, people go through the motions, half-assed, and I'm like, it's too much effort if you're not that into it. I don't want to do all this and *not* be intense. But you. O'Shay, you're incredible. Maybe in the past, with other people, it's been sometimes. And with... one person... maybe a lot of the time. You're all the time. All the time, O'Shay. Those sledgehammer tingles."

This was the start of TruthCouch.

We called each by last names because we had been public school teachers together once. Fresh out of college, all high ideals and poorly directed passion, grading every scrap of paper and never sure what to teach on Monday. We were the young teachers all the kids loved, the ones whose classrooms were filled after hours, the ones kids opened up to and came back to see, year after year. They loved us and we loved them back, loved them to an extent our degrees in psychology and social justice had not prepared us for. We would volunteer for the worst committees, coach sports after school, endlessly pass each other in the hallways as we fielded questions from kids and delivered high-fives.

"Good morning, Ms. O'Shay."

"Morning, Mr. Foster."

Subtext. Subtext, subtext.

The last name habit was with us still, a living remnant of a time when we were lovers in stylized combat, two lions on the front lines. People found it endearing, I think, although my friends' wives maybe less so than most. Even then, it was evolving into a private usage, our last names, gasping them as we locked into each other, a whisper before falling asleep. Last names then. First names in public, and never on TruthCouch.

"When did you know you were into me?"

"Oh, please, O'Shay. That's not even a little hard. One of those days last March? When it would get so cold but be so bright? We were going around making fun of all the kids' new little love affairs. *Spring has sprung! Spring has sprung!* This is all so clear. You were walking across the quad, wearing those pants with the pin-stripe and that green sweater that made your breasts look like the most amazing—"

"Ohmygod. *That sweater.*"

"-and you were walking with all this purpose and seriousness, all that sun coming down on you, and I forgot I had like thirty seconds to make copies and get back to third period, and I just stood and watched you."

"I can't believe our relationship is because of that sweater."

"And the sunshine, and your long legs."

"But really, the sweater."

"Right, but for you? When did you realize?"

"There's no ask-backs!"

"One time."

"No ask-backs, Foster."

"O'Shay…"

She sighed, gave a little laugh. "Fine. But look, it was different for me. I didn't have your great singular moment. You just seeped in, like DDT, or something in the water table."

"Gee. How special."

"No, but really. I started sitting next to you all the time at staff meetings, or thinking about some kid-story to tell you. Like, thinking about it way before I saw you, or before we had time to talk. You made me laugh all the time. But realizing it… I don't know. I guess I was talking to my mom about school stuff this one time, and she said: *Well what does Foster say?* And I realized I'd been talking about you *so much*. Then that happy hour. Then I didn't look back."

We feel in love like this. Not on the well-planned, well-executed date nights, but here, on no-account Wednesdays, eating my fledgling cooking and getting naked on the brown couch I'd inherited from an old girlfriend. We'd point at the salty streaks and laugh, fold into each other and ask questions that came with hard answers.

"What would you do to me if you knew for sure I'd be into it?"

and

"What would've happened if you never got in the cab that night?"

and

"Tell me something cruel. Something cruel you did."

She lied to me once.
On TruthCouch. She lied.

She wasn't a teacher anymore by then, joining a philanthropic venture capital firm as a jnior partner. I never fully understood what the firm did or how it kept doing what it did, never mind what exactly she did all day, but I did understand it was the perfect compromise between what she wanted and what her family wanted from her.

I was out of the classroom, too, making that move into the front office. Middle school vice-principal. Nothing else made even a little bit of sense. A vice-principal. This is work where getting lied to is pretty much written into the job description. Elementary kids aren't savvy enough to lie well and high school kids don't give a shit, but the 12-year-olds I spent my days with lied like most people breathed. Lied about who did what to who first. About where the stink bombs came from. About whether or not those girls were really making-out in the bathroom. I'm no expert in body language or adolescent psychology, and I'm not a natural in these things, but the day-in, day-out made me more attuned than most. You pick up on the rhythms and the pauses, hear the gears click as they try to build something plausible.

Like the time she lied.

"What was the biggest mistake you almost made? You were on the brink, but pulled back."

We had been out that day. It was a Sunday, still early, and we'd come back from brunch. She hated brunch. We ended up on the couch because there was something about the moment you let go of the couple-face you show in public: the first names, the prodding each other to tell the good stories, the little permissible touches. There was something so sexy about stepping out of that performance, slipping through the door and back into the less public versions of you.

She pushed me, hard, into the wall. We barely made it to the couch.

"A mistake?"

"An almost-mistake. Something that matters."

She curled tighter, pulled my arm all the way around her.

"It was that second summer, when I was in New York—remember Foster? The summer I interned and finished my dissertation you road-tripped with Joe? You sent all those incredible emails, like from a different city every time, the only way I knew where you were. Those emails waiting in my inbox, and I'd curl up with the laptop and read your words. I'm crazy about you, baby. I still have every one...

"But that summer. God, I was working so hard, stupid hours, all the time. Institute hours. I'd run with my cousin Emily at five in the morning, then at the office for like twelve hours, then work on my thesis until I fell asleep. Papers all over the bed. We never talked less. Remember?"

I remembered.

"Fridays I'd be so exhausted, two happy hour drinks and I'm out. Sunday was dissertation day. Lit review, typing out those transcripts. Saturday was the only day I ever had to do anything normal or free. I'd do retail therapy with my cousins, go on these long runs, run as far as I could go and then let the subway take me back.

"And this one Saturday, I don't remember the day exactly, this one Saturday Emily's friend takes us out on his boat. And it's this serious boat, right? Not a yuppie yacht with a captain on, like, retainer. Em's friend is tying knots and adjusting lines and all of that. He's for real. We spent the whole day on the water. You remember me telling you about this once? The booze and sun and these incredible views of Manhattan, Brooklyn, all these smaller islands I didn't even know existed.

"We got drunk, and Em's friend was hitting on me. A lot. He was funny. And persistent. The sun and the water and the whole day with him hitting on me."

She took a deep breath.

"I was tempted, Foster."

"Tempted," I said.

"Emily pulled me aside, said, *what the hell are you doing?* I knew I had to be good. Em shooting me dagger looks and I'm trying so hard to be good. I almost wasn't."

More often than not, TruthCouch got us going again—round two, or round three—the intensity of the words charging a matched intensity in our bodies. We would be spent, wearing those little post-sex smiles, and then TruthCouch, and then we would be ravenous.

That didn't happen here.

"Tempted."

"Yes. Then."

She was lying.

There was a lie in her story. I didn't know what and I didn't know where. The obvious answer that she hadn't actually been good, not at all. That this wan't the mistake-that-could-have-been, but the mistake-that-was. Those images. Sunset on the bow deck, champagne, and nine kinds of faith-breaking fucking. I was naked and she was naked and we were tangled on the couch, and I couldn't stop picturing her screwing some hedgefund dick.

But all that was too easy, somehow. If she'd carried it hibernated for this long, why risk exposure on TruthCouch? Why flirt with the revelation? It made no sense. She could have made something up. Some college sorority tale or after school special or something about almost getting in the car with him. She could have told me a different story of brinksmanship, unless-

-unless telling this, telling it here on the couch, this was the *real* story of her almost-mistake. The Escher staircase logic of it: I almost revealed my infidelity by telling an untrue tale about almost succumbing to an infidelity.

There was a clear choice. Time has since muddled the clarity, and maybe softened the urgency of it. But not then. The choice was crisp-edged and sharp, then.

I could name the lie. Or I could say nothing.

I could call it out and go after it. Or I could kiss her and make it better.

I could emperil things.

There seemed, suddenly, to be a lot at stake. At least I thought so then, laying there in the afterglow of sex and lies, and I'm not sure I've come to feel differently. Years have passed, and I don't feel differently about any of it. I still haven't changed my mind.

And we still play TruthCouch.

"What do you think about right after you pin me down like that?"

and

"What part of me do you hope they don't get?"

and

"What do you worry about that you never talk about?"

We played less and less as time went by, and now, hardly ever. The original couch is long-gone. We replaced it with the type where the stains don't show and we don't leave stains on it anyway. We don't call each other by our last names anymore either. It's technically the same last name, and our own kids are almost the same age as the kids we taught when we were teachers, back when we first met. Some of the verve of it is gone.

But life is rich, and the rhythms deep. There are trumpet lessons and basketball games, school meetings and birthday parties where adults are still sometimes allowed. We hold Sundays bracketed, sacrosanct really, for the five of us. Beach or woods or ballgame. Biking or hiking or city-exploring. There's a constructed innocence to this type of wall-building around our little family, something that reminds us to build walls even when you think you are too strong for walls.

The truth we're most interested about these days comes from the kids. Interest in them has replaced deep interest in each other. We give our nicknaming and knowing energy over to them, and dig into the three lives we made and make together. What they like, who they talk to, how they talk to who they talk to. What they think about and if they're thinking enough about anything at all. We whisper silently to ourselves, at night, before falling asleep: Please please think deeply and with urgency about things, but don't think so deeply or with so much urgency that it chips at the simple joy of these days. Please please grow into the smart and layered people we're so desperate for you to become.

I want to know all their truths.

There are times when I go full principal-mode on one of them. I slip into the old role easily, even if I'm rusty from too many years in the District Office. It works, and I usually get the truth I want. About how the lamp really broke, or how my fifth grader's teacher is teaching reading, or why my daughter is choosing werewolves over vampires. I do my old principal act with them and get the truth, but the real truth is, I wonder what would have happened if I'd done the same thing with her on the couch that day. This is what I think about as I mine the details of my kids' days, wondering what I would have learned long ago, scraping at the edges of her lie, picking at the corners until the whole thing came loose in my hand.

Sometimes, when the older kids are at sleep-overs, and the littlest one in bed, we get naked on the couch, kissing long like teenagers do. And after, we retell each other stories. Not like before, in all the hard-edged question-anwer. We stroll back, easily, through our past. Who we were, once, and what was said.

And still I do nothing when, boiling up through her tales of remembering, I hear the echo of a lie.

# What Comes
# Next Is Far
# Less Clear

# (IV)

I met James almost three years before I kissed him. Before he kissed me. Whatever. It's hard to remember who moved first, because he did, but I'd been pressing my leg against his and aimlessly scrolling through our presentation for almost two days before he finally said, "I don't wanna work right now," and kissed me. I remember thinking *oh my god this is really happening* and then turning toward him and moving my mouth into his.

We kissed for the first time in that library room, the kind you need to reserve in advance even though we didn't, kissing so long without touching really, without moving any part of us except our mouths that the motion-detecting lights went out, and then we were in the dark, kissing, still in that glass-walled room, and this was just a little too silly. He kinda leapt up and threw his stuff together and held out his hand. "Come on," he said, but it was his out-stretched hand that I remember even now, the way he held on to me that day, walking all the way back to his apartment, all the way down Burnside to his place in Southeast.

He held my hand the entire way, fingertips running along my palm and the inside of my wrist like it was the first hand he'd ever held in his life, and I think I fell for him a little bit right there, his fingers tangled in mine.

# Fourth First Day

Margot hates today. She dreads it and pines for summer like the nerd in every iconic '80s movie.

Not me. I love it. Everything is reinvented. Everything is fresh, and hope-filled, and new. Every strand of hair is perfectly styled, every cuff exactingly aligned between shoe and sock, every shoe in an expertly achieved state of tied, untied, or partially tied. The kids are coming back from summers of adventure or summers of drudgery, the air all kinds of jittery electric. They're all checking each other out, seeing who got taller and who got breasts, who got the new hair color or the new group of friends. The teachers are more or less doing the same thing to the other teachers.

I love the first day.

It's my job today to stand in the quad and appear welcoming and vaguely helpful. This is called *yard duty*. Tomorrow it will be my job to stand in the same place in the same quad and appear watchful and diligent, poised to prevent misbehaviors. An incomplete list of the misbehavior I will prevent includes:

1) running
2) chasing
3) kicking soccer balls
4) smacking handballs
5) throwing footballs
6) anything with balls really
7) taking food out of the cafeteria
8) arriving on campus without the uniform
9) screaming
10) screaming especially if you are a newly minted 8th grade girl who acts as if everyone wants to hear your voice, even though the most casual of observers could easily discern this is a thinly veiled defense mechanism to hide the fact you are afraid no one wants to hear your voice or pay attention to you at all, ever
11) Also: bullying and fighting

I am friendly. I smile and say *buenas dias* again and again.

Ramon lumbers up to me, wearing three shirts and a black hoodie even though it's already eighty-one degrees. We do a fist-pound and he tells me he's happy to be back at school because his summer was hella boring.

Here comes Lupita, looking like three years older. Not in a good way. She hugs me longer than feels comfortable, tells me I don't look as white as last year, and bounces off.

Rodney and I do the three-slap-fade-away-jump-shot-follow-through greeting we've been doing for the last two years. It looks amazing. It causes awe in everyone who sees it. He tells me he can finish in traffic with his left hand now. This better be true. I castigate him for failing to grow three extra inches like he promised he would last June.

Señora Buenuelos calls me *maestro* and hands me a paper plate with roughly two pounds of tin foil wrapped around it. *Pupusas con queso,* she says. *Para tí.* I thank her and say hi to her daughter, last year's Fs-to-As reclamation work. Geraldine looks on like she'd rather clean latrines than watch me talk to her mom in my piss-poor Spanish. For the next four months she will come into my room to hangout every morning.

Mrs. Johnson walks deliberately through the quad, dropping these withering looks at any student who shows abundant signs of life. That over-the-bifocals glare has been intimidating kids for at least two generations. Teachers, too. This is her 27$^{th}$ first-day, and the only one in which she will say *good morning* to me.

The kids swirl around us, a cytoplasmic clump of black-and-white. Dickies, collared shirts, a ubiquitious black hoodie on the last day of August. They flow and merge, unevenly sized groups, clustering in corners, staying away from the center of the quad, choosing to sit in, on, and around the peeling green picnic tables. *Let's go walking*, they say, and they leap off the tables or peel themselves off the walls, beginning the loop around the buildings where the classroom doors are open to the elements and the circling kids. They are monochromatic fish, endlessly swimming to no purpose. Because it's what they can do.

Then the bell rings.

"Everybody's on-time the first day!" Principal Hoffer bellows with a smile.

Tomorrow he will shout: "Everybody's on-time the second day!"

Make your own inferences about what he will shout on the third day.

In my hallway, the math teachers make the kids line up outside the doors. The math department is organized and does things like this in lock-step unity. It's equally admirable and gross. Only two Language Arts teachers require the line. I am not one of them. I hate the line.

"We hafta to line?" they ask me.

"No, no, no," I say. "We don't need a line! We are too strong for a line!"

Then I wave my arms in big come-in-please windmills.

Across the hall, Mrs. Alexander (6th and 7th grade social studies) is angrily shouting her first angry shouts of the new academic year. If Vegas kept a book on teacher behavior, I would have laid a month's salary on these angry shouts coming in the first five minutes. And I would have made serious bank.

Next door, Mr. Velasquez is repeatedly making kids line up. He has a lining-up rubric accompanied by old-school polaroids of level-1, level-2, and level-3 lines. He'll do line practice for like three days, and pretty much nothing else. Mr. Velasquez and I don't really kick it much outside of school.

In the quad, Principal Hoffer is issuing faux exasperated bellows: "Late? On the *first day*? I don't believe it. I *cannot* believe it!"

Standing at her door two rooms down, Ms. McDermott (7th grade math) is shaking hands with her students, and when they don't grip firmly enough or fail to make sufficient eye contact, she sends them to the end of the line until they get it right. If I did this sort of thing on the first day, or any day really, I'd be universally condemned as hella sketchy. Ms. McD gets away with it because she is:

1) Female
2) Twenty-four
3) Smoking hot

When my welcome grin starts to hurt, and my come-in-please windmills threaten to dislocate my arms, I head inside.

Inside, the room looks stellar.

Desks are in perfect paired columns. The Do Now activity is on the board and the materials they need to complete the Do Now activity are on their desks. The carpet is as clean as it will be until this time next year. No crumbs, no gum wrappers, no cockroach corpses—just the three stains that are as familiar as childhood friends.

*Stain #1*: Just to the left of the door, when Miguelitos ran in during lunch two years ago and planted an entire tray of nachos face-down on the rug.

*Stain #2:* Close to my completely un-sat-in teacher desk, three-and-a-half-years-old, when Mando tossed me a nearly full purple Gatorade after practice, having decided it wasn't all that important to actually put the lid on.

*Stain #3:* Barely six months old, the baby of the group, almost perfectly centered amongst the columns of desks, where Vanessa projectile vomited for almost a full minute last spring, the longest uninterrupted string of puking I've ever witnessed. And I was in a fraternity.

The room didn't always look this stellar.

Forty-eight hours ago, bludgeoned by an unwieldy hangover, I stood in this exact spot and was completely unable to find the productive. This was the first of two teacher workdays, paid time devoted to meetings and room set-up, and I was hurting. No one would ever know it from the level of stellar inherent in the finished product, but it's possible that there are no currently employed teachers as bad at this as I am.

This is not an exaggeration.

I set-up classrooms the way old people fuck.

I put a CD in the boombox I've had longer than most of my students have been alive, fill some pencil boxes with supplies (but not all), plug in the printer, grab a Kleenex box and put it down not where it goes, throw more supplies in the pencil boxes, drink some fast-cooling coffee, turn on a fan, pick up the Kleenex and move it closer to where it will eventually go, hang some posters (but not all), and wander around outside for awhile. Over the intercom, principal Hoffer calls us to a welcome back staff meeting. This is never a particularly enjoyable meeting, even without the hangover. It is improved only marginally by the bagels and fresh coffee and Ms. McD's long legs in little shorts.

When the meeting ends, I go back to standing and staring at the room. I move a plant, rearrange some of the desks (but not all), replay the songs I missed while I was otherwise engaged at a welcome back staff meeting, drink more coffee, throw out some trash, open the whiteboard marker containers, and finally get the Kleenex box where it goes. I trade witty text-banter with Margot, who works in an office with complimentary sushi and no teenagers.

The intercom squawks and Mrs. Johnson calls us to a Langage Arts department meeting. This meeting is infinitely worse than the welcome back staff meeting. I am argueably more hungover, there are no bagels, and no Ms. McD's legs in her little shorts. And just for the record: looking at Mrs. Johnson's legs would take ten years off my life.

I return the next day less hung-over but equally unproductive. There are eighteen hours until the kids re-arrival, and the room is very, very far from stellar. I send panicked texts to ever former student in my contact list, making dramatic promises of pizza and Jamba Juice if only they'll come to school and help set-up the room. Four kids eventually show up. Seventy-five percent of the showing-up kids are last year's co-captains from our astonishingly successful girls basketball team, and one hundred percent of today's stellar is the fruits of their labor.

A few minutes before the second bell I relocate the whispering kids to the front row, cheerfully ignoring their muttered protests, and begin our first first-day activity.

The goal here is to get them to arrange themselves in reverse alphabetical order by last name. Fast. Competition fast. I do the reverse alpha thing because I have this half-assed theory that so many teachers arrange kids in alphabetical order it creates a self-fulfilling prophecy of expectation and attention for the kids whose last names land them in the front row, and simulatenously relegates end-of-the-alphabet kids to the dregs of attention and classroom hierarchy. I'm going for a massive educational paradigm shift in the first three minutes of class.

Or something.

I sell them on the competition of the whole thing, their class versus my other class, with the best time earning fabulous prizes. This is false. The fabulous prizes are Otter Pops, and they'll be handed out to every single kid from both classes, and I'll do it on whichever day is most miserably hot, or whichever day finds me fresh out of planned lessons, and never mind my chest-thumping competitive stance today. The Otter Pops are currently cramed into the staff lounge freezer, covered in post-it notes which read:

*These are soooooooo not yours*

Or: *For kids. Not teachers.*

Or: *Back off my Otter Pops bitches*

Still, some will go missing, and I can't help but preemptively blame the math department.

Inside the room the kids are trying to do the reverse alphabetical order thing. Without talking. Fast.

There are really no words for how funny, how awesomely and consumingly funny it is to watch a bunch of twelve- and thirteen-year-olds try to arrange themselves in *any* logical or coherent way, much less an arrangement bound by the constraints of reverse alphabetical order by last name. They mill about, looking at each other awkwardly, some of them glancing at the post-it notes where they've written their names, some of them edging closer and closer to the door, a few fired up kids trying to direct traffic and get people in the correct seats. These future salutatorian-wannabees scold Alvarez, Guillermo and Anderson, Laylani for sitting in the front row, hissing: *"Reverse* order. A's go in the *back."*

I stand near the whiteboard and grin. I am massively, and strategically, unhelpful.

The best part, the real reason I do this—and never mind attempts at paradigm shifting and equity of seat-order attention—comes when they're finally seated, wearing matching aw-hell-what-next looks. Holding my roll sheet scantron, I walk slowly down the the columns, calling out the names of the kids who *should* be in that spot. They get the first couple right. Everything after that is a hot mess.

I point at a boy in the fifth desk. "Villaverde, Yasmin."

"No!" shouts Valdez, Julio, and we all have a good laugh.

After some reshuffling, I point to another kid. "Torres, Paul."

"No!" shouts Temple, Monique, and we all have another good laugh.

I could do this all day. It never gets old.

Soon, I hand out the greatest welcome back letter ever, talk about the school supplies few of them will bring with any regularity, administer a reading test because enrollment in the $7^{th}$ grade doesn't mean anyone can read like $7^{th}$ grade. Then the next group of kids comes in, needing to be herded through the door with big arm gestures because they just spent forty minutes practicing lines with Mr. Velasquez. Here is another group of kids who will be awed by how stellar the room is, who will fail to put themselves in reverse alphabetical order very well, who will stuff welcome back letters into backpacks and whine about taking a reading test.

I love the first day of school.

And I get to go home early today because there are no meetings, no practices, no tutoring sessions. I need to meet with zero parents for behavior conferences. There are no forms that need to be filed at the District Office because they lost the first two forms I sent them, no room clean-up, no after-school detentions. Just a final bell, the kids whooshing off campus like the expulsion of a long-held breath. I steer my car through the scalding Oakland streets, hit the 880 ramp and I'm on the Bridge in no time, beating the ridiculous commuting crush. I get to the short Duboce ramp without stopping once, and then I'm pulling into a fantastic spot pretty much right in front of our building on Dorland, a few short blocks from Dolores Park. This never happens, except on the first day.

Because it's Margot's least favorite day, my work clothes go in the closet and not on the back of a chair, the dishes get washed instead of ignored, and I head to the store instead of the couch.

Bi-Rite is packed, and I'm wishing I could grab a beer and a book, open the window by the fire escape and just... sit. Beer and new David Foster Wallace stories and sitting. Especially the sitting. I'd do that without the beer or the stories. My feet hurt and my right knee aches. My back too, a little. These are the first-day pains that quickly turn into first-week pains, needing to get used to all that standing, all day standing, getting used to it all over again. I know it's coming, but knowing I'll head home every day with tired feet and a sore knee doesn't change how gross all this is. I'm achy and brittle at twenty-six.

I shop fast on my throbbing feet. I buy avocados and tomatoes and bell peppers, broccoli and carrots and zucchini. I buy the Fuji apples I like and the Jazz apples

Margot likes. I don't buy raspberries because they don't have enough fuzz. I buy fresh tilapia and those pre-made crab cakes Margot can't seem to get enough of. I buy organic compostable coffee filters, cereal, and the good tortilla chips. I ask if they give teacher discounts because I always ask, even when I know the answer.

"That's a shame," I say. "Teachers are important."

Then I get real ambitious and hike all the way down to Papalote, stand in line forever and buy a jar of the best salsa in the city. The will and energy to do a 12-block round-tripper just for salsa will not reemerge until Spring Break, at the very least.

At home, I get the beer, but don't touch the chair or the Wallace stories. I start dinner, cooking the fish with garlic, cilantro, and lime. I plop a can of black beans in a pot and spice the hell out of them. I split an avocado, dig out the pit, widen the hollow with a spoon, and fill it with the Papalote salsa. I put the avocado halves on a plate with some of the chips, and set everything on the hallway table where Margot will see it as soon as she walks in.

I'm flipping the tilapia when she comes home, already eating the chips as she walks into the kitchen. Margot always looks taller than she is, long legs and good posture and never high heels. She just cut her hair, chopped and cropped like some revitalized Gatsby jazz baby thing. It looks amazing.

"Nice Finn. Nice."

"Darling, it's only the beginning."

Today, when I'm sure it hit mid-80s in the city, Margot is wearing a knee-length black dress, fishnetty tights, and clunky shoes.

"Really?" I saw, moving the spatula in a 12-6 motion.

She shrugs, eating chips and salsa and avocado, one arm tucked under the other.

"I'm not saying you don't look good darling, cuz really, you're stunning, always, but doing all that black in August? And *today*? I nearly died today. Think I ruined another shirt."

"Seemed appropriate. *Today*."

"Looks like you're all funeral-bound."

The fish is browned, and I transfer it to the oven to finish, something I learned from watching *Top Chef*. I put tortillas on to warm.

"For sure, Finn. Wish I had my hat and veil."

My banter-tone and her banter-tone are not congruous. I step away from the stove. She's set the plate on the small kitchen table and is unwinding her scarf.

"Who died?" I move toward her. I want to kiss her throat.

She keeps me away. "Who do you think?"

I laugh and she doesn't laugh.

"This day, Finn. Every year. This day."

"Margot."

"No. Really, this is the day."

I don't know if I should filibuster this, try to banter my way out of it, or got for a serious discussion of work-life balance.

"Today is the day, and like, thanks for the chips and salsa. Papalote, right? But don't expect me to be thrilled and bubbly, regardless."

"This year will be different. Hell, last year was different."

She starts to say something, but I talk over her.

"Do you know how much *better* I am at all this? How much more *prepared* I am? It'll make the whole thing so much smoother. I'm gonna roll, darling."

"It won't be different because *you're* not different."

"No, no. Look, Margot, I won't be staying up late figuring out how to teach vocab, I've got a system for the essays, I can-"

"Are you coaching?"

"Yes."

"Are you doing that task force thing for the EL-whatever?"

"ELD task force. Yes. They asked me to be the teacher-lead."

"And Saturdays, too?"

"No. Not as many. But we're piloting this program-"

Margot puts her hand across my mouth, fingertips on my lips. It doesn't matter that she started sad and is moving toward angry, there's something so sexy about her long fingers.

"See?" she says. "It doesn't change because you never change. You get better at teaching, and like, it doesn't take as much out of you, and then you go take on something else. Something from there. Always from that place, and never from me or us or anything else. I'm behind that school, behind Hoffer, waaaaaay behind your kids. First come Juan and Maria and Jamal. Then me. Maybe."

"Margot."

"No. You're alive with me for two months, and a ghost for ten. Today is the day I always become a widow."

"First you'd need to be a wife to be a widow."

"That was *not* the right thing to say, asshole."

She leaves, big shoes making all kinds of noise on the wood floors, and I need to get the fish out of the oven.

The first thirty-seven times we had this fight I followed her and put my arms around her waist, resting my chin on her shoulder and whispering promises in her ear. I held her close, my chest against her back the way she loves, and said all the things she wanted me to say. I did this in bedrooms and kitchens and hallways and city streets. I made promises I knew, even as the words slipped from my lips, that I couldn't keep. Promises I didn't know how to keep.

I don't follow her anymore.

Tomorrow Margot will be better. It's just the reaction to the first-day, all the build-up over the weekend, when I laid out the shirt-tie-pants combos that had been hanging unused all summer, when I made little piles of supplies by the door, things I needed to bring and didn't want to forget, when I talked about how funny it would be to watch the kids try to get themselves into reverse alphabetical order by last name.

The tortillas are curling and going black around the edges. I don't like how long the fish has been in the oven.

Margot's getting smacked around by all these adjustments and readjustments, the anticipated changes to me, my life-style mutations.

The transformation from Finnegan to Mr. Conner.

Finnegan smiles easily, reads the Internet to discover new happenings, starts sentences with *weshouldgocheckout*; Mr. Conner has sore feet and an achy back, has been known to fall asleep at the kitchen table surrounded by papers and green grading pens. Finnegan doesn't worry about much except the fact that you need reservations everywhere, and the crowd at the bars seems younger all the time, and maybe he should be saving some serious money sometime soon; Mr. Conner worries all the time, worries about teenagers he barely knows, worries about doing right by them after so many haven't. Finnegan tries to keep in shape a little, tries to make the most of this amazing city he's landed in, building a dynamic life for him and the woman he loves; Mr. Conner tries to use reading instruction to combat poverty and violence and generations of institutionalized racism, leaving earlier and earlier every morning to wage his daily little wars. Finnegan is still in bed when the sun comes up, still there to hold and be held.

Today Margot mourns for Finnegan, who will make the occasional cameo, but won't be back anytime soon.

Tomorrow she'll feel better.

Tonight the fish burns and is ruined.

# What Comes Next Is Far Less Clear

# (IX)

After the whiskey stopped working, there was only the shavasana.

The whiskey was, of course, the first thing I tried. The night we ended, splitting apart with the slow-moving inevitability of a forest fire, I threw my helmet down the stairs and rode my bike through empty city streets, reckless and cold. At home there was whiskey in a stamped bottle, and I sat in a chair by the door. Maybe I dozed off, but mostly I sat and drank and then I changed my clothes and went to work and pretended that nothing was wrong at all.

No, nothing all.

Didn't sleep so well.

Tried that new Thai place. Maybe a mistake.

There is a unique form of self-destruction to all this. When the person you love no longer loves you, not *never* loved you, but loved you once and no longer, crossed that particular finish line and then turned back around in the opposite direction, hands stretched out in that *whoa, sorry, my bad* way, when you become a person who is at once capable of inciting love but at the same time a Keroauc-style Roman Candle unable to sustain it, causing the person you love to resort to a type of logic Aristotle would have used if he watched way too much reality TV, offering this explanation of I-love-you-but-I'm-not-*in-love*-with-you, investing that difference between *love* and *in-love* with a significance that tastes suspiciously like vomit, when you are told (again by the person you love), that you are the cure for these short years here, but not the longer and more profound ache that stretches inexorably forward for the many years to come, when you are told these things you try to destroy the *you* that lies at the center of all this.

Because to live as someone like that would be unthinkable.

There are hundreds of ways to dynamite the insufficient *you* out of existence, but almost all of them were too blunt for what I wanted. That type of surgical extraction required a precision insturment.

I chose whiskey.

For a long while I thought it had been a good choice. Even though they talked about me at work (repeated outfits, dishevelment, thousand-yard stare), the whiskey was doing exactly what I wanted, helping close-out the impossible hours beween coming home and becoming unconscious, helping blunt the recall of unhelpful dreams. Then it stopped working. Suddenly, and at once.

I couldn't bridge the gap between the front door and sleep. I couldn't keep from waking up. I couldn't stop remembering everything, all at once, all the time.

And then I had only the shavasana.

I agreed to try all this with a *what the fuck* shrug, hauled my weak-ass body through pose after pose, stiff and sore and clumsy. I sweated alcohol and night-terrors onto a borrowed mat, sweated through the few old t-shirts that didn't remind me of anything. It was only after an hour of this self-inflicted trauma, when we were called to lay on our backs and I tried to regain my breath, palms facing the ceiling in that strange awkward bend, it was only then, in those few minutes, that the hurt really stopped.

And who knew? It worked like the whiskey once did, the shavasana. It was only then that I could quiet the march of all this awful shit, all those terrible goose-step echoes.

Twice a week became every night. And once the whiskey failed, I started going twice a day. Then three times. I found a sunrise practice halfway between home and work, a gym-class near the office. I bought one of those mats. A purple one.

"You must be getting so good!" my co-workers gushed.

I'm not. I'm getting broken.

In my ninth hour of yoga in two days, my arms can barely support a simple downward dog, much less hold crow pose. I shake and quiver as soon as we're asked to do more than a forward bend, dragging through it. Soulessly. Joylessly. I cramp all the time, sitting cross-legged, or even returning to child's pose. I cramp at my desk, too. My hip is not working right, and I limp, noticeably. I do this little compensating shuffle thing down the hallways and people notice.

I arrive at a practice, kick off my shoes, and start watching the clock. I'll do everything they ask but all I want is the shavasana, the corpse pose. All I want is the three-minute reprieve when I can step out from under the weight of my own insufficiencies like Atlas passing off the globe for just a second. Here, yeah, can you hold this for a sec? Thanks. I can do this, I can, but I need those brief moments of unburdening, unyoking, and then I'll carry it forward.

I wait for the shavasana and the globe-passing, even though I know there's not one thing about this can last, and there's not one thing left to try, next.

# We Are Almost Always On The Verge

**PART I:**
*Finals Week*

**From:** sam.michaels@gmail.com
**Sent:** Wednesday, May 7, 2006
**To:** kerrick@bc.edu
**Subject:** RE: getting our drink on

my last final was actually today, and i'm
taking off back home, so i can't make it out.
if i don't see you before you head off, good
luck. it's been a hell of a ride, and man,

this thing you're doing is incredible. drop
some emails, let us know how everything
works out.

sam.


**From:** sullivant@bc.edu
**Sent:** Wednesday, May 10, 2006
**To:** kerrick@bc.edu
**Subject:** RE: getting our drink on

T-Rav,
Good times at MA's last night. No doubt
you're getting a lot of these things, but
happy trails and all that. I'm not gonna
lie, you'll be missed, kid. Partying with
the 3rd floor Ignacio crew won't be the same
without ya. Peace, brother.


**From:** casey1@bc.edu
**Sent:** Saturday, May 10, 2006
**To:** kerrick@bc.edu
**Subject:** sorry!!!


I totally didn't mean to get that drunk! I
was a hot mess! All I remember is getting in
the cab and just completely breaking down.

I'm so sorry. I wanted to have this grand
goodbye, but the vodka-redbull killed all
that.

Seriously Travis, you've been my mid-term
savior. I don't know what I'm gonna do next
year without you. A pint of Cherry Garcia
and Travis's lecture notes… I love you
adopted little brother. I love Claire. I
love what you're doing. Don't you dare be a
stranger. Miss ya already.

Love,
Lauren


**From:** postaldave@hotmail.com
**Sent:** Saturday, May 1C, 2006
**To:** kerrick@bc.edu
**Subject:** RE: getting our drink on

dude! listen im drunk outta my gourd right
now and im trying to make sense but im
probably gonna fuck it up but its gonna suck
working at o'brians without ya thats it. btw
im blacked out right now

**From:** dkerrick@mkm.com
**Sent:** Monday, May 12, 2006
**To:** kerrick@bc.edu
**Subject:** FYI

Travis,

Your mother and I are leaving for the
Hamptons early this afternoon. I trust you
know the number of the house there, and of
course we will have our phones with us. We
expect to hear from you this weekend.
Dad


**From:** carsonp@bc.edu
**Sent:** Wednesday, May 14, 2006
**To:** kerrick@bc.edu
**Subject:** final paper

Dear Travis:

I've just now finished my final reads of the
intro papers this weekend; thank you once
again for your excellent preliminary work. I
have also finished your own final, which is
tremendous. You exhibit not only a firm
grasp of the material but also the ability
to draw strong analytical lines to the

germane foregoing thought. The ability to
make these connections, as well as the
quality of your conclusions, is far and
above what I expect from somone of your age
and experience.

On a slightly different note, I have been
thinking about the plans you shared with me
regarding your future, and I feel the need
to echo, and perhaps underscore, some of the
comments I made earlier. You have made great
beginnings here, and I feel there is very
little limiting the paths ycu could travel.
Far be it for me to question the choices you
are in the process of making, but I fear
that such a change has the potential to
undo, or at least undermine, much of what
you have worked to build here. Think of the
difficulties inherent in developing new
relationships, learning new ground. These
seem like lateral movements at best, do they
not? There are also disparities in
institutional quality to consider, which are
real, and not the product of east coast bias
or ivory tower smugness. Can you not wait?
From what you've told me, you both have
already waited. Two years, yes? Is there no
way to delay until next summer, or even next

spring? If I've over-stepped, forgive me. My age and the name on the door tend to bring that out more than I'd like. Come by Monday if you can. We should speak more.

Best,
Peter

Peter Carson, Ph.D
Director, International Studies Department
Boston College
Gasson Hall 109

**From:** dkerrick@mkm.com
**Sent:** Wednesday, May 14, 2006
**To:** kerrick@bc.edu
**Subject: re:** re: FYI

Travis,

Suffice it to say you two-sentence email was grossly insufficient. I'll be on campus today. Expect me by late morning.
Dad.

**From:** omarvas@gmail.com
**Sent:** Saturday, May 17, 2006
**To:** kerrick@bc.edu
**Subject:** the last charge of Wyatt Earp and his band of immortals

Vis,

I woke up this morning, fuzzy-headed, thick-tongued and immediately experienced a sense of horror I haven't felt since rolling over and coming eye-to-eye with that girl from the Reserve Desk freshman year. Some things are better left unsaid, so let me just say I remembered with horror that you'd left today and I wasn't on hand to help throw shit in the trunk and stand on the corner as you headed up the hill at Comm Ave and away. I wasn't there and it sucks.

(I should mention, maybe, that this is the second time I've done this; failed to say goodbye when the goodbye mattered, and although I was able to bomb down 93 in the rain last spring, racing the ruptures in my father's blood vessels and arriving only after Last Rites, enough time to scream and cry and refuse to be comforted, today there was nothing to do but head out to Lower for a stir fry sub and appreciate the short skirts the warm weather has wrought.)

Last night was good, the manycoldbeers was
good, but there are things you say on the
corner, right after helping pack the trunk
and right before you hit the top of the
hill, and I didn't get to say them.

I can only begin to fathom the forces that
are pulling you away, but really are pulling
you *toward*, and wonder from the distance of
incomprehension how you did it, keeping
those forces whole and intact through the
last years. I mean, no, really, how'd you do
it? You've got this answer here to everyone
who questioned the paths that took you away
from what everyone else was always doing, an
answer to how all those nights were spent,
alone and not alone. You have it now. I can
only begin to scratch at the surface of
understanding.

Which makes it hard to go on. The scratched
surface understanding makes it hard to keep
writing and harder still to find the right
way to end. This introspection gets harder
not because of unwillingness but maybe
because of something fostered by
unwillingness, made thick and dense and
unscratchable by unwillingness that builds
up like scar tissue or big, long, sweeping
rings of moats that get deeper as they move
closer to the border. Eventually, they crowd
the castle and flood it with unknowing and

wash away with their mute flow everything
that was there of value, so that nothing's
left in the castle but a vast empty tower
and crumbling stones that are weeping with
the water from the moats, and with the
desire to have something behind them to keep
warm and protect for when the battles come.
And the stones whisper at things you're not
sure you want to know because if you knew
you'd want to build moats around them.

So I'll say this, what I should have said
but the freshly-packed trunk: You've been my
friend, and there's almost nothing that
means more.

You're going after the one thing that does.

~Omar Enrique Vasquez

# PART II:
## *Late Summer*

The last time Travis saw Claire she was standing
on the little jut of lawn in front of their apartment,
wearing a spring-green dress that swirled around her
ankles. They were more or less face-to-face, in the

aftershocks of the last few days. The car was packed, and he was leaving. He was leaving to points unknown. This was partly by design and partly because he wasn't sure where to go.

They were sometimes looking at each other, and sometimes taking elaborate care not to. This was harder for Claire because she did not want to look at his car, either. She could see the duffle bags filled with his clothes and the mik crates filled with his records, and she did not want to look at any of it.

It seemed like no one had said anything for a long time.

Then Claire said, "Your mouth looks like it wants to tell me something."

Travis kind of physically abosrbed the remark. He was *Trav* to most of his friends, *Vis* to the best one, frequently *T.* to her, and he shrugged into her words the way you absorb a jostle on a crowded street. Then he kissed her, and this was not something he wanted to do.

It ended the night before.

There had been a three-day conversation. It began when she walked in the door after a night spent away. A night when she did not come home and did not call and Travis had waited up, drenched in the hot grind of shame. The next morning she walked through the door pouring a story of unplanned drinking and cell phone dying and passing out on a friend's couch and feeling terrible about the whole thing.

Travis:

listened.

Claire:

over-told and over-explained, layering in detail to prove how true it all was and it seemed as if she knew it but couldn't stop.

Travis listened, deciding not to:

share his own details or tell her about the waiting up, staying awake through the heavy mid-western summer stick; explain how he had left the windows open all night, letting in the sounds of drunk undergrads on their homeward stumble and the howls of neighbor cats, the ones that sounded like someone was putting a blowtorch to the feet of small children, the ones that sounded like sounds that were welling up from some clenched place inside him that wasn't even supposed to be able to make sounds.

Travis decided:

these were his details and he could keep them to himself.

Claire:

stood by the front door, hair pulled into a messy ponytail, hands forward, apologizing.

Travis did not:

share any of the lurid events that could have explained
her absence; did not share or attempt to explain the
insignificances she had created; say anything about the
howling cats, and how he felt he understood them a
little, those cats and their howls; tell her these things; let
her explain and move on.

It was only the beginning. They spent three days
building this talk, laying bricks on the foundation of her
explanation and his reaction. It was impossible to stop
talking. They walked out of rooms with sentences half-
finished. They started again, later, in the car, or the
shower, or the back aisle of the little organic grocery they
went to every Saturday. Reaching for produce.

"It's just, what if *I* were to do that. What then,
y'know?"

"If I've been restraining you."

"No no, no."

"I'll stop right now, if I'm holding you back from
something you want."

"No, no."

"Because sweetheart, for sure, the last thing I
want is to box us in to something we're not. It's the last
thing, completely."

It was a seventy-two hour talk, more or less
completely without pace or structure. It was what they

talked about to give voice to everything they weren't talking about.

"It's fine. This time. It's fine, but I feel myself waiting for the next time."

"The next time, what?"

"The next time, when I come home and you're gone, and I'm wondering if this is the next time."

"I feel like I'm supposed to say don't-worry-Travis-that-will-never-happen."

"I feel like I'm supposed to be more angry about this time."

It was a talk kept disjointed to restrain the panic. Under the words, underneath the plot of their talk, they both knew something that could not be true. Not remotely. Not for them.

### Travis did:

talk about how worried he was that her night of not coming home could have only one explanation, the awful cliched obvious explanation; share his fear of a someone-else somewhere, a fear somehow more accute now that he was actually here, and not separated by the distilling effects of 800 miles and a timezone.

### Travis could not:

talk about his deeper fear that more and more he was seeking a pattern to his days he knew she would never appreciate, that his desire for staying-in nights of cooking and couches would be stiffling; or tell Claire that her capacity to be enthralled and wounded and affected by every small thing created expectations he probably could never live up to.

Travis did not want to know:
what that said about him.

Claire did:
feel betrayed by his suspicion.

Claire did not:
talk about the growing possibility that the thought and lure of Travis she had nurtured across the years, across the lonely night of improbable fidelity, that this idea was somehow greater than the reality of him in her bed, in her arms, underappreciating; or let him know she was seeing herself in a new way, as someone who, just maybe, built grand fantasies in place of reality.

Claire did not want to be:
a girl who could fall into the stereotypical trap of liking-the-thought-of-the-guy-better-than-the-actual-guy.

They could not stop. They could not find a way to finish. They walked out of rooms with sentences half-said. They changed subjects or fell into silence, talking the thing dry.

Until the third night.

On the third night, seventy-two hours after she walked in the door with explanations on her lips, Claire made the halting, knife-wound diagnosis, and Travis did not resist.

She said it was over, and Travis closed his eyes and nodded twice. They did not know what to do next. This was suddenly the biggest problem in the room. What to do next.

Claire was on the bed with her legs tucked beneath her, staring at him. She was sitting with hands clasped like someone trying to remember how to be good. Then she moved across the bed and put her hands on his zipper. She rubbed with her palms and the heel of her hand, all these little eliptical movements. She tugged at his belt and could not get it off, yanking and making a sound that was equal parts moaning, laughing, sobbing. Claire tried to see herself in this new way—a woman grabbing her newly *ex*-boyfriend's cock and crying at the same time.

She gave up on the belt and pulled at Travis's shirt. He undid the buckle and buttons and zipper. She took off her top, leaving the skirt. She hiked it to her hips, waiting for Travis to grab under the elastic and pull her underwear down to her ankles.

There were no words for sex like this. Falling into each other and sliding across the planes of hip and leg, bed and floor. Claire did not stop crying until it was over, lifting her face to press against his, smearing the wetness from her eyes down his cheek and neck and shoulder, and putting her mouth again and again to the damp places.

The guilt:

came after.

It had taken three days to reach this measure of clarity, however unthinkable. This ruined it, smudged the crispness of the decision, their guilty relapse fuck.

That feeling again, kissing in front of the apartment.

Travis kissed her:

because standing with a woman like this, in the sprinkled sunshine of an early morning like this, made not-kissing almost impossible; because her head was tilted at that angle and her little jutting mouth drove him crazy almost always; because there was a part of him that truly believed that kissing her now and like this had the power to fix the slipping, ruptured parts of them, would somehow cause them to shake off the silliness of the packed car and the leaving, and go back inside, make love on the couch, and laugh over breakfast at how close they had come to ruining everything.

Claire kissed him:
because no decision or three-day talk could change how fundamental it felt to be kissed by Travis; because this was still her most natural state, his mouth on her, her fingers curled around his neck.

Claire could see:
the car on the other side of his bent head, the records in their crates, and then she remembered.

Claire kissed him:
because there were only so many times she was capable of turning away from him, and she still had one more left to go.

## PART III:
*Saturday, May 17, 2006*

Claire woke up naturally, letting the alarm clock go un-set, and this was something she almost never did anymore. She lay on her back in the too-big bed, elbow out, hair spread across the pillows. She woke up laughing in a dream, and heard the echo in her head as she slowly opened her eyes, the remains of the sound still on her lips.

She was waking up in slow graduals, looking over the room. *This is my room*, she thought, and swung her legs off the side of the bed.

Her room, so carefully arranged, brought her a sense of comfort she knew was a little silly. She spent too much time on the displays of shell-candle-dried flower, or the groupings of potpurri-bowl-tiffany-lamp-picture-frame. She knew it, but that knowing could not erase or diminish the well-being that gripped her every time she walked into the room. It held her and kept her close every time she lay sideways on the bed, touching her cheek to the velvety comforter.

In the kitchen, she poured orange juice from the container, nearly emptying it, and sat at the table in the little enclosed porch, drinking the juice and watching the glass.

Travis was coming today.

She pictured him readying the car in the gray Boston dawn, the inevitable Dunkin Donuts coffee sitting on the roof as he loaded up the trunk. She saw him in real time, driving those ridiculous streets, a city he loved, and one she'd visited so many times she thought of it as hers too, just a little. She saw him taking the turns by the Charles as the sun came out, as the city began to wake, saw the morning light on all that old brick.

He was twelve hours away and Claire wondered if he could see her. She wondered this often, if he could see out of her eyes, or see her through the eyes of others. There were times she felt him so strongly, holding so tight to her heart, that it seemed impossible he wasn't caught in the same way, that he wasn't sitting in class or out somewhere equally affected by her.

She drank her juice and wanted more as soon as the glass was empty. The kitchen still looked strange to her. The living room still looked strange. She had been taking things off walls, clearing space, emptying the apartment so Travis could come and help her refill it. The kitchen had been yellow, but she had spent the last few nights going over it in primer because she could not imagine Travis standing near yellow walls.

She had skipped a study session, and she had bailed on their weekly *Veronica Mars* viewing. "Claire can't come out," Lindsay said after psych stats. "She's nesting."

Her room she had not changed, and this bothered her. Soon it would need to be *his* room as well. She could take the frames off the walls, get rid of a small table or the chair that never really worked anyway, but she couldn't change her room. The space resisted every effort.

She sat there in the sun, still wearing the robin's-egg scrubs and white top she always slept in, tasting the acid-juice aftertaste on her tongue and knowing that as soon as she got up—maybe to fill the glass, maybe to leave it in the sink—as soon as she moved from this spot, here, it would be an end to all the ceaseless waiting that had gone before, all that had been faded and washed out with the near impossible hope that soon Travis would be here to refill the emptiness she had intentionally produced, recreate it for her with his voice and new eyes, recreate everything really, and she would be in motion, finally, done at last with the half-starts and the almosts, the useless paused time she had lived and now disposed of, rising up and into the lovely churn of all the days ahead.

# Thanks:

to Scott and Sean and Paul and Mel and Carl and Nikos and Lisa for letting me talk about this in bars.

to Jose Vilson and Kasia Cieplack-van Baldegg and, especially, John Holland for taking the (uncompensated) time and energy to design a cover that matched what I saw in my head.

to Mike, who took an amazing photograph that fit these stories so well, and if that wasn't enough, gave me a chainlink fence to tear apart when that was pretty much exactly what I needed; to Jim, who put words together in exacting, incredible emails, and didn't take offense when I repurposed his words and life story a little; to Glenn, who seemed to instinctively know which two phone calls, two years apart, were the necessary ones; to Maureen, who taught me things and showed me things I might never have otherwise known—particularly the meaning of loss.

These things matter.

Probably a lot.

# Kilian Betlach:

has educated kids in urban communities since 2002, and had his life changed teaching other people's children;

lives in San Francisco;

rides a bike;

likes his whiskey;

also wrote *This Feels Like A Riot Looks* (a novel), *Teaching in the 408* (a blog), *Teaching 2030: What We Must Do For Our Public Schools Now and in the Future* (a collaborative teaching book).